Who owns all the oranges?

by

Oran Burke

Who owns all the oranges?

Copyright © Oran Burke 2014

www.oranburke.com

First published June 2014

Oran Burke has asserted his right under the Copyright, Designs and Patents Act 1988 to be identified as the author of this work.

All rights reserved. No part of this publication may be reproduced, distributed, or transmitted in any form or by any means, including photocopying, recording, or other electronic or mechanical methods, without the prior written permission of the publisher, except in the case of brief quotations embodied in critical reviews and certain other non-commercial uses permitted by copyright law.

The characters in this book are fictitious and any resemblance to actual persons, living or dead, is purely coincidental.

Cover design by Jess Hillier

ISBN 978-0-9572689-3-7

For my parents

We thought, because we had power, we had wisdom.

Stephen Vincent Benét
Litany for Dictatorships, 1935

Who owns all the oranges?

"I met Mr. Kane outside. He said they came again last night," Cassie said as she walked through the door and flopped onto a chair in the living room.

"Yeah," I said.

"What did they want this time?"

"Oh, the usual, do I still think the way I did ten years ago, am I a member of any protest group, what colour is my underwear?"

"Dad!"

"Sorry sweetie, it's just getting a bit ridiculous now, that's all."

"Why are they still doing this if you haven't done anything wrong?"

"It's more about letting me know they're there."

"Why?"

"The kind of things I used to write are not appreciated anymore. They want to make sure I understand that and don't get involved in anything."

"Are you?" she said, getting up to go to the kitchen.

"What do you think?"

"I don't know anymore, what we're taught at school suggests that anyone who ever disagreed with the government should be shunned."

"Is that what counts as learning these days? Are you going to spurn your father because of his supposed mistakes?"

"I guess not," she said, smiling as she walked back in with an apple, "but it is a bit confusing. I sometimes don't know what's right or wrong anymore."

"That's not unusual at your age you know. You're still

growing up, trying to work out the world for yourself. True, life in today's Britain can be a bit bewildering but you're just going to have to get on with it I'm afraid."

"That's not really the puzzling part. I remember hearing you and Mum talk when you still lived at home. You often spoke about how things were in the old days, how you wouldn't have had to go through all of this just to do your job."

"You were much younger then, maybe you didn't understand everything."

"Yes, but I'm seventeen now so you can probably stop patronising me. I think I'm old enough to get it."

"Perhaps it's time we chucked you out on the street to fend for yourself as well then."

"Hah hah, you're so funny."

"Alright, settle down now. How's your mother?"

"She's fine."

Cassie ruminated for a few seconds before speaking again.

"Dad?"

"Yes, my dearest darling daughter?"

"Why are things the way they are?"

"How do you mean?"

"You both talked all the time about politics and the economy and how bad life was getting for people, or how much the country had changed from the one you grew up in. I don't really get it, what's so different now?"

"Some of it is just age sweetie. People often yearn for more carefree times, which tend to be when they were younger, but the last thirty years or so have seen some big changes in how everyone lives. We don't have the same opportunities we once had. It depends on your point of view I suppose, but I think we've moved in the wrong direction."

"How?"

"The increasingly wide gap between us and our rulers, both socially and financially, or the lack of faith most people have in the organisations that are supposed to protect us. Those ideas weren't always so ingrained. It's hard to pin down to specifics but having lived through the shift, it's difficult not to feel a bit nostalgic."

"That's what I really don't understand. I've heard almost nothing about this glorious past and at school we learn about the splendid present, so I can't connect the two. It's like everything that happens to you. I sense something isn't quite right and I constantly feel like bad things are going to happen."

"I think you should worry more about your final year in school, which isn't too far away."

"Why, there's not much to look forward to afterwards."

"What do you mean? You'll be off to university hopefully and ..."

"Don't change the subject. Why won't anyone tell me?"

"Who have you asked?"

"Just you and Mum."

"Ok, let's keep it that way."

"Why?"

"Don't worry about it. Just don't go questioning people too much about this sort of stuff."

"See, that's the problem. All you ever say is not to

worry about it. It's like I can't think for myself. You've always said you need all the information to see the truth. Why is this different?"

"That's not what this is about. It's just ... better if you don't know."

"Really? I've lost one of my closest friends and my father disappears regularly, sometimes for days at a time, just to point out a couple of things I know for sure. What frustrates me is why. Why are you the enemy?"

"I'm not the enemy Cassie. I'm just another convenient scapegoat."

"See, let's start there, I've no idea what that means."

"Cassie, why do you think I get bothered so much? It's because I know too much. I don't want to put you in the same position."

"I can take care of myself."

"Maybe, but this is different."

"I wouldn't tell anyone what you told me."

"I know sweetie, I trust you. That's not the problem."

"Then what is?"

"No matter what I tell you, there will always be information out there that will try to disprove what I'm saying. I'm not sure it's going to help you deal with anything."

"Dad, I need to decide what I'm going to do for the rest of my life sometime in the next few months, and everything we get taught is about what we can bring to the future of the country, what part we can play in the next great steps of our nation. How can I decide what the best choice for me is if I don't understand exactly what kind of place I'm supposed to be working for? Shouldn't I know what I'm getting myself into?"

I sat thinking for a few moments.

"Ok. Look, I can tell you but there are two conditions."

"What?"

"Firstly, you never tell anyone. Not your mother and especially not any of your friends. I think it's right that you know so you can make up your own mind, but there are not that many people around that admit to knowing this stuff anymore and it can mark you out as being different, and that's enough for the authorities to ask questions."

"Ok. And the second?"

"You have to listen to it all, every last thing I say. If you want to know why The Stability System exists, then I'll tell you, but no getting bored and giving up half way through."

"Ok, I get it."

"I hope so."

"Dad, don't worry. I've listened to the way you and other adults talk about this too many times. It's always in hushed tones and quiet corners. I get it, it's secret. It's a bit dangerous. I have to be careful."

"I'm beginning to think you should have spent more time asleep when you were younger and less sitting on the stairs listening to conversations that weren't your business."

"Then how would I have ended up the well-rounded individual I am today?"

"Shush now smart-arse, and make your father a cup of tea."

"So where do we start?" she said, getting up to put the kettle on.

"With democracy."

"Oh, that again."

"Come on now, it's important, that's why I've told you a bit about it before," I said, following her into the kitchen and sitting down. "I know it's judged now as being unnecessarily cumbersome but at one time it was considered the best way of doing things. It was never perfect, but it was as close to fair as it could be."

"But surely now we've stopped using it, it no longer has any relevance to how we live our lives."

"Actually, that's not quite true. It's a question of history. You need to understand the last system and why it was discarded before you can understand the present one. You're forgetting that democracy, after universal suffrage in the 1920s, survived for nearly a hundred years and the basic principles had been in use for centuries before that."

"What's universal suffrage?"

"Well, suffrage is the right to vote in an election and the universal part came about when women were given the same rights as men. From then on people accepted it as the best way of giving everyone in the country a say in how things were run. Sure, it had its faults but the basic theory of electing a representative for a group of people who would bring their thoughts, hopes and grievances to a central decision-making body was a sound principle. You understand how the country is run now, right?"

"Uh-huh."

"But you also know this system hasn't been in use for very long."

"Yes, yes. What I don't understand is why you think it's so bad."

"Because I, and everyone else of my generation, grew up with something we consider better."

"That doesn't answer my question. Why?"

"People had some say in how Britain was governed back then. If you chose to vote, or protest, or sign a petition, you could at least say your views had been recorded and you'd taken an active part in the running of the country."

"Can't we still do that? I mean, people still get to vote at least."

"Not in the same way, not at a national level. You do citizenship classes, don't you? How do people make their opinions heard?"

"I don't know. The Central Cabinet make decisions about what's best for the country."

"And what if you don't agree with what they decide?"

"I hadn't really thought about it."

"Nobody does anymore."

"Fine, but in school we were taught that it was too slow moving and restricted the ability of the country to prosper."

"That's a very simplistic view but unfortunately one that also has an element of truth. It wasn't necessarily the fault of the system though, just how it had been applied. It took hundreds of years to get to a point where everyone was able to have their say, so in some ways democracy was just a blip in the history of Britain."

"A century seems like more than a brief change."

"Perhaps when you're seventeen but at fifty it doesn't seem so much. To put it in perspective, the first steps towards democracy were taken in the thirteenth century. It took more than seven hundred years to get to universal suffrage but less than a hundred for it to disappear completely. Maybe it's flippant to describe it as fleeting but the amount of time, thought and effort it took to get to a point where everyone could have a say seems wasted now. How much is written about all this in your school books?"

"Maybe half a page or so."

"And what did your teacher say about it?"

"Not a lot, he said we only really needed to be aware that it was the old method. It comes up now and again, but not in a very positive way."

"Doesn't it surprise you that a system developed over hundreds of years only gets mentioned briefly when you're learning about how the country works, especially as it was still in use until about a decade ago?"

"I guess that's a little strange, but isn't the point that it's discredited now, that it's no longer fit for purpose?"

"Well, that's for you to decide."

"Why don't they say more about it in school?"

"I think we'll probably get to that at some point. We should really start with the Magna Carta though, the set of thirteenth century documents which set out the principle of the rule of law."

"What's that?"

"It meant that everyone was entitled to a fair trial and no one was above the law, technically not even royalty. That may not seem important now, but the principle whereby anyone could be sent to jail was the first step in saying that everyone was equal, even though it only applied to an elite group at the time. More than four hundred years later the Bill of Rights strengthened the idea that people should have certain privileges enshrined in law. It was essentially the beginnings of what used to be referred to as civil liberties."

"What's does that mean?"

"That you have to ask that question is part of the problem. They were the freedoms the population as a whole had that couldn't, or shouldn't, be taken away. They were never really written down in one place but were made up of a bunch of things like the Magna Carta, the Bill of Rights, new laws, traditions and sometimes even just historical writings from the past that helped develop our ideas of democracy."

"It sounds a bit disorganised," Cassie said as she put two mugs of tea on the kitchen table and sat down across from me.

"It was, and it might have been a good idea to write it all down in one tidy document the way other countries did, but in fairness they often based their constitutions on the lessons learnt here."

"But we have one now don't we?"

"Not one that sets out the rights of individuals with respect to the state, which is what most do. Ours is a vague wishy-washy document that makes no real promises and was only written to pseudo-legally do away with history. It has no bearing on our ability to hold our rulers to account or any connection with what were once our rights."

"So why did democracy fall out of favour?"

"It's more complicated than that, it was more that it gradually became less acceptable to those who governed. It's hard to pinpoint where exactly its demise began, it often depends on who you speak to. Historically, it may have started with Margaret Thatcher, the Prime Minister in the 1980s, but that's so long ago that most people have forgotten the details. She certainly pushed the ideology of market forces shaping the country and went to war with the unions."

"They were responsible for destabilising the country according to our history teacher. Isn't that why she had to defeat them?"

"What you're taught conveniently ignores the growth in poverty and inequality that took place in the eleven years she was in power, something that is still with us today and has plenty to do with the anti-union stance she promoted. While it's true they were unpopular because they often held the country to ransom, that was no different to banks saying they were too big to fail when the 2008 crash happened. There are people still alive today who hate Thatcher for the way communities were ripped apart by her actions, but equally there are those who think she improved the country immensely by dragging the economy into the modern age. Because of her electoral success, the opposition found themselves gradually coming around to her way of thinking, which led us to where most people remember the demise of democracy beginning – when the Labour party took over in 1997."

"What was that again?"

"It was one of the two main political groups that tended to win elections in the late twentieth and early part of this century. The other one was the Conservative party, often called the Tories. In theory they had very different views about how the country should be run, but in the mid 1990s they started to become more similar, as they were both very business friendly when traditionally only the Tories had been, and Labour had sided with unions and workers. Anyway, after about seventeen years of Tory rule, a guy called Tony Blair led Labour to a huge victory."

"That name's familiar. How was that a turning point for democracy?"

"Well, it wasn't immediately, and really it was the combined efforts of Thatcher and Blair that prompted its downfall. He carried on her inequitable economic policies, and then added a few undemocratic twists of his own. In those days the cabinet was much the same as it is today, made up of the ministers in charge of departments, except they were elected, then chosen from the party which had a majority. The British government was in theory run by consensus, where the cabinet would discuss major issues facing the country and try and solve them together. Over time Blair began to lose interest in this and turned to advisers instead, meaning decisions about the country were being made not by a group of MPs but by unelected staff, something that was called a sofa government."

"A what?"

"It was a term used to describe a less formal way of running the country, sitting around with your aides deciding policy rather than doing it the more formal way of consulting with ministers. There was nothing necessarily wrong with having a close group of advisers and discussing issues with them but they seemed to become more important in Blair's government. Don't get me wrong, he wasn't the first to do this, but he took it to a different level, probably because he fancied himself as more of a US-style president than a British Prime Minister."

"Couldn't he do what he wanted? Isn't that what democracy was, politicians making decisions for the people."

"I suppose so, but it was a representation of it which didn't conform to the traditional view."

"I'm not sure I understand. If he had been elected surely it was his right to do things as he saw fit."

"Yes and no, the rules and traditions of British democracy allowed a certain amount of autonomy for the Prime Minister but there were also restrictions on the role."

"Like what?"

"There were four main ways he should have been held to account, by the public, press, parliament and his own party. Also, the judiciary had a say in the matter because in those days anybody could take the government to court to challenge something considered against the rule of law."

"That seems like a lot of ways to make sure he does what he should."

"Well, yes, but think about each one. Public opinion would show up in elections, protests and polls; freedom of the press was considered necessary so all politicians could be held to account; parliamentarians and political parties were in danger of being voted out of power if they didn't support the rights and views of people. So the theory of democracy is very good, it's just that in practice it relies on the goodwill of politicians not to push the limits too far."

"And this Tony Blair did?"

"He did, but within the rules. Every government has done to a certain extent, no matter who was Prime Minister, but things seemed to get more high-handed under him. Once he got things started, it was easier for those that came after him to keep the laws already in place and in some cases expand them. Don't get me wrong, he did some good things as well, it's just the bad things were very bad."

"Such as?"

"He's remembered mostly now for the Iraq War."

"Oh, we did something about that in school. I knew I recognised his name from somewhere."

"Really, what does the Department for Education have to say about it?"

"That it showed the value of a strong leader."

"Interesting twist, but not entirely accurate. Firstly he sent troops to Afghanistan after the attacks on New York in 2001. This was generally seen as ok as the scale of what happened was shocking to people who lived in Europe's relatively secure bubble. When the case was made for going to war in Iraq two years later, public opinion was against it unless there was United Nations support, which never came. There were huge demonstrations, and many of his own party refused to back him, but he went ahead anyway. He cajoled parliament into voting for the war and presented evidence that was eventually proven to be seriously flawed. How many innocent civilians died is still disputed, but it was a lot. By the time US and British forces withdrew more than eight years later, one monitoring organisation had it at well over one hundred thousand, but those were only the ones they could confirm. It was probably many, many more."

"That's terrible. Why are you telling me this?"

"It may seem like I'm digressing but it makes an important point. Think again about checks and balances as they used to be called. The public – ignored, the press debates – ignored, his party – ignored. The only bit that supported him was parliament, and that was only possible with the backing of the opposition, which was a little embarrassing for a Prime Minister with a majority. He stifled debate by cutting the time given over to cabinet discussions, ignored the public and press and relied on the opinions of a select group of advisers.

It was just one of a number of things that started during the Blair years. After 2001, the nature of democratic countries didn't necessarily change immediately but there was a sudden openness about the nasty things they were willing to do."

"How do you mean, nastiness is normal now?"

"That's true and the regulations brought in were similar to what happened during The Emergency. In some cases they succeeded and sometimes the bills were toned down from their initial harshness. Laws that dealt with terrorism, which had been passed to deal with the troubles in Northern Ireland, were adapted to allow longer detention and easier deportation of foreign nationals now they wanted to target Muslims. In the ten years or so that Blair was in power, it was like two steps forward, one step back when it came to the government's desire to be more draconian. Laws came in, were repealed, adjusted, strengthened and scrapped, but the overriding effect was a removal of the rights of certain people to a fair trial. If you look at it in today's terms, it became acceptable then to control the movement of people they considered needed to be watched.

"That was just the stuff that happened within the country of course. Britain, the US and several of their allies were mixed up in the kidnap and torture of people they suspected were involved in terrorism. Now, these things had probably always happened, it was just done secretly before. This time the US in particular was open about the fact that it had a prison where they kept people without trial. Over the years, stories eventually came out about how people got there and it turned out that many of them were seriously abused, not necessarily directly by Britain and the US, but more than likely with their knowledge. The governments dressed it up in words like extraordinary rendition and enhanced interrogation, but it was just kidnap and torture. The problem was that because of other bombings in Bali, Madrid and London, a lot of people justified these things or ignored them, effectively endorsing them."

"Dad, I'm not seeing where all this fits into the end of democracy."

"Ok, let's go back to everyone having the right to a fair trial supposedly being one of our guiding principles, something that was understood the world over but not necessarily always adhered to. By not standing up for the rights of the individual, Blair and his government devalued the Magna Carta and the Bill of Rights and took away any moral high ground they might have had to criticise other countries. That's not to say we held that territory convincingly to start with, but by stating openly that they were choosing to ignore international conventions, they began the process of dismantling their ability to lecture others. Do you see what I mean? If you present your nation as a standard by which others should treat their citizens, and then you take part in a dubious war that causes the deaths of tens of thousands of innocent people, or get involved in the same unsavoury acts you've criticised other countries for, then you lose all integrity. At the time, international human rights organisations were criticising Britain and the US in the same way they did the most brutal regimes in the world.

"And don't forget, just like today, when you make this kind of behaviour normal, people will try to defend it. There were arguments in pubs and living rooms across the country about whether any of what was happening was justified. The problem with forcing people to take a position on such ethically unsound practices, done in their name with their tax money, is that out of a sense of patriotism people will defend it, regardless of the long-term harm it does to the country's image or its democratic principles."

"So there was some support for what happened."

"Of course, in those days there were always a number of viewpoints and debate about the issues of the day was still allowed. Remember though that war was only one of a number of things that happened in the early part of the century that led us to where we are today. It was also when surveillance cameras became a normal feature on our streets."

"But that's no different to now."

"No, but the uses have changed. Originally they were used as a crime deterrent. Public opinion quite rightly fell on the side of prevention and they became commonplace across the country, eventually making British people the most recorded in the world. Again, it was just one of those things people got used to and there wasn't really any harm in it when used correctly, but when something offers the possibility of misuse, it will be exploited by someone. Facial recognition technology has now advanced so far that it's possible to pinpoint a person on a camera and automatically track their movements for as long as you want. The comment politicians used to make about the explosion of cameras was that if you weren't doing anything wrong, you had nothing to fear from them. These days the language has altered subtly to describe them as necessary for the stability of the state, and that has more to do with the people who have control than anything else. Whereas before they were considered a protective force for good, now they've acquired a more sinister use. If anyone knows that you do."

"Yeah ... I still think about Iqbal sometimes."

"I know sweetie but you see what I'm saying, don't you? It was easy to use selective camera evidence to claim his cousin was involved in something dodgy and then round up the rest of the family individually using identification software."

"He was my friend. He didn't do anything wrong. They just grabbed him off the street in front of us. I still don't really understand why. Will all this stuff you're telling me help explain it?"

"I'd like to say yes, but I'm not sure it can."

Who owns all the oranges?

We had always educated Cassie about politics and the world outside, though with increasing care as chaos flourished around us. She was an inquisitive child and we encouraged that, considering what we taught her about life to be complimentary to her schooling. As time went by however, it became less and less acceptable for parents to teach their children anything that might contradict the preferred doctrine of the Department for Education.

This became uncomfortably clear in early 2020 when I was called into her school. Cassie had come home a few days previously and said, 'Daddy, what's democracy?' Aside from the difficulty of trying to explain the intricacies of the British version to a seven-year-old, I wondered why she'd asked and it turned out her teacher had said during a history lesson that it might not be fit for purpose anymore.

I learned about the workings of government as a trainee journalist on a local newspaper and felt strongly about the ongoing corruption of its principles. We were in the second year of emergency powers, but there had been no indication that children's education would now include the suggestion that our right to vote might be removed. I told Cassie why I thought this was wrong and was surprised to find myself in front of her teacher and head a few days later.

"Mr. O'Dwyer, we need to speak with you about your daughter, in particular regarding some of the obstructive ideas she's been putting forward in class," said Mr. Greaves, the head teacher, a stressed-looking man in his fifties who seemed like he might be more comfortable anywhere but running a school.

"Go on," I said.

"Well, it seems last week she contradicted Miss Caulder by telling her she was wrong about something that had been taught in class. We are of course all for individuality but there needs to be some restriction on the disruptive effect this may have on other children."

"Can you be more specific? You seem to be telling me there's a problem without saying what it is."

"I'll let Miss Caulder explain the details."

"Thank you Mr. Greaves," said Miss Caulder, a tall woman in her mid-twenties, probably not long out of training. "This isn't necessarily the first time Cassie has been outspoken and we were hoping to try and impress on you the effect this might be having on the class as a whole."

She stopped talking, as if expecting a response. When none came, she continued.

"At the end of last week I taught a short interactive history of the nation as required by the syllabus. It consisted of a simple representation of how the country is run but according to Cassie you took offence to a comment I made regarding the usefulness of democracy as a governing system. As she put it, 'my father said you're wrong'."

"Offence might not be the word for how I felt. Maybe disgust."

"Perhaps," said Mr. Greaves, "but I think the issue is more to do with your undermining of Miss Caulder's work."

"I understand what you're saying but what you said to her is untrue so I would question why you were making comments like that at all. If Cassie has been disobedient or disrespectful then I'll most certainly talk to her, but what you're asking me to do is lie. I suspect if you go out on the street and ask twenty people whether they'd like to give up voting, most of them

would agree with me. When I heard what you said, I chose to teach my daughter what I think you should have in the first place. I'm a little surprised that given you should be teaching a curriculum, you're bringing your personal opinion into the classroom."

"It is the curriculum ..."

"I think what Miss Caulder means is that we are obligated to provide all viewpoints to give a rounded education," said Mr. Greaves.

"Sorry? Let's just go back a bit. Are you seriously saying it is now policy to teach children that their future might not include the ability to choose our government? You're teaching this to seven-year-olds?"

Mr. Greaves shifted uncomfortably in his chair.

"The most recent advice we've received from the Department," he said, "is that in light of the last couple of years of instability, we need to be balanced in our appreciation of the fluidity of the situation and how we impart sensitive information to the children we teach. We have also been asked to provide guidance to parents."

"Telling kids that they may not have a say in how the country is run when they're older is firstly probably over their heads, as evidenced by Cassie's questions when she got home, and secondly, doesn't even begin to give them the truth. It's nothing more than slightly disturbing brainwashing."

"That's a very strong term and not one we appreciate. This has come from the highest level and I will not have you sit in my office and accuse us of indoctrinating young children."

"Fine, but that will have no bearing on what I teach my daughter at home. If the government choose to try and push *propaganda into the minds of children in a manner worthy of the crassest dictatorship, then I will counter that at home, for reasons of balance of course."*

Mr. Greaves frowned at me while Miss Caulder inspected her feet.

"Mr. O'Dwyer, I'm not sure your tone is helpful," he said. "Our worry here is that divergent viewpoints in the classroom will confuse the children."

"No, your worry is whether the Department gives your school a good rating or not and I'm assuming that is now dependent on you pushing the ideology laid down by them. I sympathise with the fact that your jobs are affected by this but I cannot agree with the corruption of my child's education. I've listened to your guidance so you've done your job but if this kind of teaching is to become normal, I will educate my daughter about the realities behind the spin."

"Very well Mr. O'Dwyer, there's little else to say then," said Mr. Greaves, getting up and smoothing himself down. "I would however ask for your understanding of the effect these ideas may have on the other children. Please ask Cassie to refrain from discussing these matters with her classmates."

I chuckled involuntarily.

"Is something funny Mr. O'Dwyer?"

"She's seven. How is she going to understand any of this?"

Mr. Greaves looked at me and indicated the door.

The following day I did what any self-respecting political journalist would and wrote a piece about the whole encounter, wondering aloud why children were being taught a dangerously callous doctrine and questioning whether government education policy was heading in the right direction.

"Dad, you home?"

"In the garden."

"Hi there," I said as she popped through the patio doors, "how was school today?"

"Fine, the usual. What are you up to?"

"Just relaxing in the sun. I haven't much work on this week so I've had a lazy afternoon."

"Nice for some."

"There's a jug of lemonade in the fridge if you want some."

"Ooh, yeah. Back in a minute."

"Hang on. Bring me a refill," I said, handing her my glass.

"Ok."

She came back a minute later, put the glasses on the table and sat down.

"What's up with you?" I said, "You look troubled."

"I've been thinking about the things you told me last week and it still doesn't add up. I can't see how we got from those few changes to where we are today."

"Ok, but I did say those were just the start of what happened, and," I said, dropping my voice to a whisper, "we shouldn't really be talking about this out here."

"I know, sorry. I just wanted to say, that's all. Anyway, it's only Mr. Kane next door and he wouldn't say anything, would he?"

"Who knows? Probably not. Don't forget there's a footpath the other side of that wall as well. You want to stay for dinner?"

"Ok, but I have to help cook, you're rubbish."

"Hey! Watch your cheek."

"Alright, I'll go and ring Mum and tell her."

When she got back we sat in the evening sun for a while talking about what she might do when she left school, before moving to the kitchen. As we made dinner, she looked up from chopping carrots, her face screwed in concentration.

"Dad, why were they allowed to get away with it? Why didn't anyone do anything to stop the government if there were ways to hold them to account?"

"That might be the most complicated question of all. Pointing out what politicians are doing wrong doesn't necessarily mean they listen. The simplest answer is some people did speak up. There were plenty of protests but in the end the majority accepted that the gradual restrictions placed on their lives were necessary because they didn't seem like limits at the time. You don't subdue people by taking everything away at once. You chip away at things, slowly sculpting the system you want or need, or you control the flow of information so no one realises the scope of what's happening. That way, everyone gets used to each measure before you introduce the next. Also, Britain has historically been a fairly subservient country, where the elite ruled. Voting was originally only for a select group that was expanded gradually up to the point of universal suffrage. Most of the population had no say in how the country was run and merely worked for their existence, not much different to today. In some ways it made the removal of long-held rights easier."

"I'm not sure I understand."

"The gulf between ruler and ruled is almost a national tradition – monarch and subject, a Parliament of barons and working serfs and more recently the fascination with what class you were born into and whether you were being true to it – all of these things are part of the us and them, have and have not mentality that's obsessed Britain for a long time. It's difficult not to see it like that when even after everyone was allowed to stand for election, most of the government, regardless of ideology, tended to come from top schools and universities, essentially keeping a system of minority rule in place. Of course there have been exceptions along the way but not so much that Parliament would be representative. Over the years the country has watched politicians vie against one another in the Commons, with all its manufactured conflict and childish behaviour, and because of its unrealistic nature and lack of connection to everyday life people developed a disdain that eventually made them indifferent to it. Perhaps it was that which led people to be more accepting or uncaring about Stability."

"Ok, but I still don't get why the government at the turn of the century thought the best thing for the country was to start ignoring rights that had been in place for centuries?"

"That wasn't really their intention. I think most politicians involved believed they were doing the right thing to combat terrorism, but it turned out to be at the expense of our civil liberties. The problem was that around that time, lack of detail became normal in the passing of laws, and life in general. When new bills were put before parliament they often hadn't been analysed to make sure they weren't open to abuse. Policies were announced that sounded great in newspaper headlines but when it was time to put them into practice, scant initial research left them open to interpretation. The emphasis, very much begun with Blair, was that style mattered more than substance but if you look at things like RIPA, it's obvious his government should have spent a bit more time thinking about the legislation they brought in."

"What's RIPA?"

"The Regulation of Investigatory Powers Act. It was passed in 2000 and was supposed to regulate surveillance by government bodies. The problem was the wording allowed a lot of flexibility and appeared to have been provided by the security services to make their lives easier. Eventually it was used for so many different things that it became a standard for how badly legislation could be written. The proof of that is how readily The Central Cabinet embraced it."

"So what did it allow?"

"Oh, all kinds of things. Councils used it to see if parents really lived where they said they did and the security services eventually used it to set up a massive spying operation on the old internet. I was working on a local paper at the time and we talked a lot about what it meant because we were often the ones breaking stories about how organisations were abusing it. I mean, it was a wide ranging law that covered so many things in so vague a way that it was always going to be misused."

"Why did nobody speak up about this?"

"Journalists did but it was hard to get the general public to take any notice. Firstly most people thought it was a bit of a dull subject that didn't apply to them, and secondly the IRA bombing campaigns of the 1990s were still fresh in people's minds so the government were easily able to pass it, and other laws around that time that dealt with terrorism, as the final push for peace in Northern Ireland. Then, the attacks on New York happened so it looked like it was a necessity."

"Why were the security services listened to so much if they weren't elected? Why were they allowed to write the law?"

"In theory they worked for us, the people who provided the taxes that paid their wages, with oversight from MPs who we elected. Their job was to protect the country from attack from inside or out and one of the agencies that existed before they were merged, MI5, was even officially charged with protecting Britain's parliamentary democracy from subversive organisations. That really meant extreme left and right wing groups whose stated aims were the overthrow of the state, even though they were unlikely ever to have the power to do that, and after the fall of the Berlin Wall those groups more or less fizzled out. The problem was that the security services then spent a decade without as much to do, their budgets were cut back and some people were openly questioning what we needed them for."

"Why?"

"You've done a bit in history about The Cold War haven't you?"

"Yeah."

"When the Soviet Union disintegrated, the threat of a nuclear attack from the east disappeared almost overnight. This was seen as a victory for our shared western values, effectively Capitalism versus Communism in its most simple but inaccurate terms. I'm too young to remember a lot of this but for more than thirty years, people were constantly nervous about a conflict breaking out that had the potential to wipe out large sections of the world's population. The death and devastation that could have happened were frightening and once that threat disappeared, some asked why we needed elements of the security services anymore. However, there was still the question of Northern Ireland so they kept some of their powers, and after Blair signed the Good Friday Agreement, he appeared to let them dictate the terms of how they would ensure peace stayed in place. It was in his interests that it did as it might have been seen as a personal failure if it hadn't."

"So RIPA brought in the supervision that happens today?"

"It wasn't so much the law itself as how it was used, and what happens when there are people in power who exploit it for the wrong reasons. There was always some form of surveillance, just not on the massive scale that happened when the internet took off. Once there were a few points that could be monitored, GCHQ, the listening service, found they were able to access more than they ever thought possible and that was the beginning of everybody being targeted, rather than specific people who were suspected of doing something wrong and RIPA made that legal. So in the same way that cameras are now used to track everyone's movements, data collection became a way of sifting through the content of everybody's lives. Of course, most people didn't know about it until 2013 when a guy who worked for the US government leaked a huge number of files detailing how much was actually being recorded."

"Did people not get angry about their privacy being invaded?"

"Not really, at least not in Britain. I think a lot of people assumed that all internet communications were being monitored anyway, so it wasn't as shocking as it could have been. They just got on with their lives, assuming someone would tell them if there was anything to worry about."

"And nobody did?"

"Some of the media did, but the majority of UK news organisations, including those with the biggest readership, just ignored it. In some papers, it was as if it never happened."

"But why? The press were surely in the best position to inform people."

"Yes but hindsight is wonderful and it's difficult to know what really went on. There may have been pressure put on them not to report, or in some cases there were ideological differences about the release of what were considered state secrets. Those who understood how contrary it was to our individual rights and freedoms did write about it but the debate that should have happened didn't."

"Why not?"

"Hard to say, it just never captured people's imaginations, or they never thought it could ever affect them, which if you were a normal law-abiding citizen should have been true. Even when it became obvious the government were going to support the security services in continuing as they had before, the majority of people just ignored it. Probably most chilling from our point of view today was the open intimidation of journalists. They went to newspaper offices and destroyed computers that contained leaked files, held the partner of a journalist for nine hours as he passed through Heathrow and David Cameron, the then Prime Minister, openly said action might be taken to stop further details of the files being published."

"And that was unusual?"

"At the time, yes, but it had as much to do with his ignorance of the law as anything else. All the same, press freedom was still considered an important part of a free and open society and he was ignoring that entirely. Those episodes showed that the real power when it came to information rested with the security services, who were humiliated by having their secrets uncovered but had the ear of government. That influence allowed them to say they were doing their best and the country was being secured, but don't ask too many questions. However, it's always difficult to trust organisations that have a conflict of interest."

"What's that?"

"It's an old term that doesn't get much use these days. If the security services are telling the government that such and such needs to be done to protect the country, and if telling them that will result in more power or money being given to them, then it's in their interests to continue saying the same things. So their influence is directly dependent on whether their role is thought to be important, but they control the information used to judge that. That's a conflict of interest, as it could, in the wrong hands, lead to them overstating the need for themselves, and nobody, apart from them, knows the truth."

"Ok. But if all this surveillance stuff was out in the open in 2013, then why didn't something change?"

"The heads of MI5, MI6 and GCHQ, the three organisations that made up the security services back then, were called before a parliamentary committee, which were groups of MPs that used to scrutinise the work of government. They were asked some gentle questions to which they gave some standard answers and claimed to have foiled lots of attacks on the UK, but said they weren't able to tell anyone the details for reasons of national security. In some ways, that's an understandable reaction as they weren't sometimes called the secret service for nothing, and knowledge of how they operated wouldn't have helped them stop attacks, but this method of speaking let them continue to sway government in their favour. Of course, the other side of this was that they weren't just spying on suspected terrorists and the general public. They also spied on companies, union officials and politicians as RIPA allowed surveillance in the economic interests of the UK. That let them legally monitor anyone who took part in strikes or anti-business demonstrations, or MPs who objected to the corporate intrusion into politics, without ever having to justify why.

"When the three intelligence services were merged in 2019 after the review into the bombings, they arguably gained the final piece of power they needed as when they were separate they had to individually justify funding and coordinate with each other from separate locations. When everybody had free access to all the stored data, information from around the world could be cross-referenced more easily. It gave the newly created Singular Security Service more influence on government because all three sections could now speak as one unaccountable voice, and claim in even stronger terms that what they said was right."

"Did they push the country into The Emergency?"

"I'm not sure about that though it's a popular theory. You need to look at it from a different perspective. They lived in a bubble and probably did see threats to the state everywhere but may never have intended to turn Britain into a security state, even though that's what happened. Opinions vary because conspiracy theories mature easily in a vacuum, so it's simple to say that for twenty or thirty years this was what they had been planning, but that's the worst case scenario. Remember they weren't alone in creating the system we live under but at best they were as misguided as all the others, truly believing they were helping the country and protecting it from harm."

"So RIPA and the internet surveillance programs were just part of what enabled them to take control?"

"Well, yes, along with their allies. Like I said, these things don't happen overnight so it's difficult to pinpoint when exactly they went from protector to persecutor. Scholars, whenever they're allowed to again, will probably research that question and come up with a definitively vague answer. After 2013, they certainly became more defensive about their operations, particularly those that involved handing over large amounts of data to the US. Perhaps that was when they began to see democracy and free speech as a threat to their existence."

"Didn't it trouble anyone that they were paying for this and the government was allowing it to happen?"

"I don't think it's possible to say accurately when tens of millions of Britons stopped caring about having their every move recorded, or whether they paid for it for that matter. The more important question would be whether they realised it was happening at all."

The first time I had a visit from government officials, I suppose I'd already been on their suspicious list for some time for being critical of the introduction of emergency powers, but it also coincided a little too closely with the call in to Cassie's school and the piece I wrote criticising the Department for Education.

When I went from local papers to writing blogs and articles at a national level in 2005, I still had some of the fire of youth. I moved to London, found myself at the centre of an energetic mix of people and built my reputation as a political commentator during a couple of years on one of the tabloids. Not long after, I met Jane, Cassie's mother, and we settled into a comfortable life, bought a house in southwest London and had a child.

It was probably that level of comfort that led to my surprise when I answered the door one night in February 2020 to find two earnest looking men from the Home Office wishing to have a word. I ushered them into the front room, telling Cassie to go back to bed when she appeared at the top of the stairs. Jane, a financial journalist who understood well enough what was going on, went upstairs to assure her all was well and that the men just wanted to have a chat with Daddy. This wouldn't have seemed unusual to be fair, our house was an open place where people came and went all the time. Children can sense tension though and the gloomy figures at the door exuded that.

Once inside, both men sat on the sofa and I took an armchair across from them.

"Mr. O'Dwyer," said one of them, "we're here this evening to try and negotiate an end to your unsupportive stance. The

commentaries you have been writing over the last couple of years have been unacceptably critical of some of the efforts made to improve security."

"Is the government trying to stifle the press?" I said.

"No, our aim is cooperation not coercion. It's felt that perhaps you could refrain from writing more controversial pieces until the situation within the country has improved."

"Interesting, most people's lives seem to have gone back to normal. I haven't heard about any bombings or threats recently. What exactly is unstable at the moment?"

"We can't comment on issues of national security Mr. O'Dwyer. The government does feel however that in order to maintain equilibrium, policies currently in place should be continued."

"What, the imprisonment and deportation of whole families without trial, torture, religious intolerance? Perhaps the government should try and be a little more imaginative. All that stuff is so 1930s."

The other man, who had remained silent until now, spoke.

"I don't think your attitude is helpful," he said.

"Ah, the old good cop bad cop routine."

"Mr. O'Dwyer," the first man said, "We are asking for more support for the government's efforts, that's all. We'd like you to think what effect your words have on stability. The threat to the nation is significant and I don't think you realise the damage you and others like you are inflicting on the debate surrounding detention."

"I think you'll find that if you silence one side, technically speaking it can no longer be called a debate."

"Nobody is trying to silence anything. We are merely

asking you to understand that we are living in unique times and the country needs to unite behind a single idea."

"So what I write is causing division?"

"Yes, we believe so."

"I probably don't need to remind you about freedom of speech and the press, I suspect you already know. What worries me is that you don't seem to care."

"On the contrary, the government believes wholeheartedly in a vibrant press, what we are concerned by is the apparent disregard some journalists have for the fact that we are living through a national emergency. We are at war Mr. O'Dwyer and we need to come together as a nation if we are to win."

"I don't doubt that this will mean nothing to you but perhaps some of the real wars that have been waged over the last twenty years or so shouldn't have happened. Then we might not be in the position we are now, convincing ourselves that we're constantly in conflict with a minority of a minority. Maybe we should be looking at the causes of what happened a couple of years ago rather than deciding the only way to deal with this is more confrontation."

"You are entitled to your opinion but that's certainly not a view shared by the government."

"Mushy liberal tosh," said the other man under his breath.

"Thanks for joining us again old school," I said, "but I think what you're missing is that without the existence of other opinions, there won't be any restraint on the power of the government. The elections this year need to be more informed than at any other time in recent history, given the current behaviour of our politicians, so I see it as my job to exploit my contacts in the government, civil service and

military to offer people more of the truth so they can make their own decisions."

"Well, that brings us to another point. We don't appreciate the current leakiness, particularly in the detention centres. We don't believe this is in the interests of security and steps are being taken to remedy this issue. In the meantime we'd like a list of your sources, particularly from within the military."

I laughed.

"I'm sorry," I said, "are you asking me to hand over the names of my whistleblowers so you can silence them?"

"Our current belief is that it is not in the best interests of the country to have so much information being released to the public, and as I said, we are working on reducing the flow. If you are a patriot Mr. O'Dwyer, you will hand over those names."

"You're not really from the Home Office are you?"

"Now listen here," said the silent one, "I think you need to start thinking more clearly about this. We're not going to force you to hand over those names, or tell you that you have to stop writing your particular brand of rubbish, but you need to be more aware of what you're doing to this country. This debate, as you call it, is not worth wasting breath on when we're at war. You are insignificant in all this and ..."

Good cop put his arm out to interrupt.

"Mr. O'Dwyer, please think before you write, that's all we ask," he said.

"I always do. I think you gentlemen should leave now. You've made your point."

"Thank you for your time," said good cop, while bad cop just scowled.

After they left, Jane came through from the kitchen.

"What was that about?" she said.

"I don't really know. I think it was a warning. They seemed to think I was destroying the fabric of the nation by reporting the abuses of government."

"Surely they're not trying to pressure journalists to stop writing negative stories."

"It was weird. I think they'd like it if I did but it wasn't a straight request. It was more like a message. They asked me for the names of my contacts."

"They what?"

"Yeah, in the interests of patriotism."

"Fuck."

"I know. How's Cassie?"

"She's fine, she went back to sleep pretty quickly."

"Good. I think I need a glass of wine."

"I'll join you."

We sat at the kitchen table and tried to tease out what the visit meant. They had issued no real threats or asked for any guarantees of cooperation. They had merely delivered a message suggesting I shut up.

Next day, it became clearer when I began to get calls, emails and texts from other journalists. I wasn't the only one to receive confrontational night-time visitors. It seemed there had been a concerted effort to intimidate the most outspoken journalists, regardless of their political persuasions. In the end it only made those of us who were critical more determined and those who had sat on the fence jump down on our side. A few of us met for a drink and agreed to write about it, working on the basis that they couldn't and wouldn't silence everyone and go through the hassle of being accused of trying to stifle a free press again. Many of us had worked together in some capacity for years, and although we might have diverged in our opinions and beliefs, we recognised the gentle pressure they were trying to exert and the extent to which it bothered us.

Unfortunately our open letter to the Prime Minister only got enough exposure for a few hours online storm before everyone moved on to something else. This allowed the Downing Street spokeswoman who dealt with it to say that they had merely sought the help of journalists in maintaining security, spinning it to seem like we were at fault. That episode altered the tone, making us realise that something subtle had changed in the treatment of the press and that maybe we had to be more careful about how we went about our work.

Over dinner, the conversation continued.

"So was it after 2013 that the internet was restricted?" Cassie said.

"No, that didn't really happen until the early twenties. I mean, several countries had already managed it to a certain extent as after the revelations about US and UK collusion in tracking not just their own citizens, but people and politicians in other countries as well, much of Europe decided to take control of their connections to the web. Germany was the first but the difference was that it was done to try and ensure nobody else could spy on them, not like it was done in Britain, as a means to monitor and control everyone. Much of present day Germany and many other countries in Eastern Europe lived under autocratic regimes that had closely watched their people for decades until the fall of the Berlin Wall, so they were far more squeamish about surveillance than Britain.

"Here, some sites found they were being hacked or attacked more often, then partially blocked depending on what they were publishing. This had always been possible but it took on a more sinister edge when unseen hands began to focus on dissenting voices as well as terrorism. When The Communication Protection Laws were brought in, it opened the floodgates, allowing the government direct access to internet providers and the ability to shut down an offending page quickly, supposedly in the interests of national security. We began to notice that more and more material was disappearing, including older articles, particularly when we had something to say about new restrictions, or internment, or whatever was deemed to be anti-Stability that week.

"So we tried to stay one step ahead. Most journalists became quite good at using technology after 2013, as the awareness of what GCHQ were doing led to an explosion in custom-built security software. All of that is illegal now, but I hear some people still develop and use that sort of stuff. There are off-grid technicians who roam rural areas connecting to the web anonymously, using satellite connections to download restricted data from abroad and make it available on underground networks. Even so, the large majority of people get their news from approved sources and don't forget it's not just the internet they're attempting to control, but information in general."

"Why is there an obsession with that though, what will it damage if we know what's going on in other countries, or even what's really going on here?"

"When the camps opened and elections were first cancelled, The UN, the US and most European countries were appalled that Britain, which had often held itself up as a model democracy, now appeared to be crumbling into one of the dictatorial states it had once criticised."

"How did the government here react?"

"With the same language they still use today, that a pragmatic approach to security necessitated hard decisions and all measures were temporary until the situation improved. However, the criticism only got worse, so they decided to try and control what people could see, on the slightly spurious grounds that it would improve the security situation. Worryingly, this worked, as the more people read about how Britain was an embarrassment to democracy, the more they became unhappy about the ridicule and condemnation. This could have led to focus turning on the government that caused it and ultimately to some sort of soft revolution at the very least. Who knows, we never got to find out as our access was gradually curtailed, slowly but surely removing anything that wasn't acceptable.

"In the beginning it was just material that criticised the camps and cancelling of elections, then anything that had a political edge, whether it was in support of the government or not. They seemed to become afraid of any commentary that wasn't controlled by them, as if it might lead people to think outside the narrow area of judgement they needed to foster. Eventually all websites had to be licensed and were forced to maintain servers here that only allowed users from Britain, meaning they had almost absolute control over what could be seen. By the end of 2022 there was close to nothing on our internal internet that gave unbiased information about the rest of the world. We were cut off for the most part unless you knew how to circumvent the barriers, which plenty of people did but it was, and still is, a constant battle as web routes are shut down and new ones opened. The part of the Singular Security Service that monitors and blocks the internet is now the largest employer in government. It used to be the health service, which tells you a lot about the priorities of our rulers."

As I got up to make coffee Cassie said, "Some of this stuff is frustrating. I feel angry with people for not doing more to stop the government. If more of the population had stood up and objected, then we might not be where we are today. From everything you've told me so far it seems everyone is to blame for this. Why allow it to happen? Why just sit back and allow your rights to be taken away?"

"You shouldn't be so harsh really, and definitely not so angry. I understand why you are, but you have to see how difficult it was for people to go up against them. It's not right to judge people who are faced with the might of the state, particularly when it gradually becomes more brutal and uncaring. Don't forget that people don't speak their minds so much anymore so it's impossible to know how they feel about all of this."

"Maybe, but I'm too young to have done anything about it, so why didn't anyone else?"

"What, like me?"

"Anybody! But ok, why didn't you?"

"I did as much as I could, in the only way I knew how. Hang on," I said as I wandered through to the living room, reached into the cavity behind the bookshelf and pulled out the hidden copies of articles from the past.

"All of these are things I wrote until I was persuaded to stop," I said as I handed them to her.

"Why have you still got these, isn't it dangerous?"

"There are very few places to read newspapers or websites from the past. Funding cuts had already done away with most libraries by the time emergency powers came in and when limitations were placed on everything else it was too late to make copies. There's rumoured to be a room in the British Library where banned literature is imprisoned and internet restrictions stop most other things being seen. When I realised where things were headed I started making records not just of my own articles but others' as well. A few of us have done it but I'm amazed I've still got mine. The house has never been searched because they rely on fear and surveillance to keep people in line, though any books deemed unacceptable were taken, including my own. A long time ago electronic methods won over the security service and they forgot that people still know how to speak and hide and read things that aren't on a screen. It's probably their biggest weakness. Anyway, I've become more compliant in the eyes of the government over the years and my hiding place is good so I keep them to remind myself of history."

"Why stop writing about it though, surely you should have kept trying to tell people how wrong things were?"

"It's all very well saying that Cassie, but the reality is the mainstream media were hobbled by the early twenties and most of them lacked the ability or inclination to question the government long before that. Then they started on the protest websites, slowly but surely wiping them out with fear and laws. There were very few safe places left to write."

She looked absentmindedly at the pile of paper in her hands.

"Can I read these?"

"I think you should, it might help you understand better the mood at the time, but you'll have to do it here. I can't risk them leaving the house."

"Ok, but I still don't fully understand the role of the media in all of this. I've listened for years to you and Mum talk about television, websites, newspapers and all kinds of other things related to that monster you call the media. The way you talk about the press, it's as if it was once some revered higher being that could do no wrong, but all I see now is rubbish and lies. It's even worse now you've told me what's really going on. It just seems like mindless propaganda. I can't see any traces of what the two of you talk about."

"Well, as always we have to go back a long way. I won't bore you with stories of takeovers, mergers and circulation but let's just say that the most powerful media organisations in the country used to be feared by politicians."

"Really?"

"I know, hard to believe isn't it? On the one hand there were the widely read tabloids that theoretically had the power to sway undecided voters and loved a good sex or money scandal, especially when it was a politician they were ideologically opposed to or a celebrity they wanted revenge on. Then there were the supposedly more serious broadsheets which sometimes did more investigative journalism. It wasn't exactly a golden age but I remember moving to London and thinking this was it. The money was never good and you had to work hard, but you always felt you were part of something that could make a difference if it tried a bit harder. Perhaps I'm biased because that's the kind of thing I'm interested in and it would be arrogant to think that's what everyone should read, but in its own way it was important. If government can be held to account by focussing on accuracy and honesty then it's a service to the country as a whole, whether people want to read about it or not."

"Around the turn of the century though, serious investigations started to disappear as if they didn't matter anymore, and didn't really reappear for another decade. There were some exceptions along the way but for the most part nobody was willing to put money into it like they once had because there was never a definite story at the end. About the time the Tory/LibDem coalition came to power in 2010, a number of non-profit organisations sprung up that were dedicated solely to investigative journalism, often funded by donations from wealthy benefactors or the public so it looked like a bit of balance was going to return.

"Unfortunately things then started to go a little awry because certain sections of the press, while feared to an extent, had also become complacent about their power. Politicians had been snuggling up to them in an effort to get more favourable reports from those with the highest readership but that all changed with the phone hacking scandal. It isn't worth going into too much detail but most importantly it exposed the awkward cosiness that existed between some newspapers and politicians. They'd always had an uneasy relationship because on the one hand parties wanted coverage for their policies but had to put up with criticism to get that and journalists needed a close relationship with politicians to get good stories but could just as easily be frozen out for unflattering articles.

"The ideal scenario where at least some of the press were holding institutions to account had become skewed in favour of power on both sides. A few papers, both local and national, continued to fulfil that role quite well as they were often the only people in courts, Parliament and council meetings though budgets couldn't stretch to covering everything so they often had to be selective about what they reported. The problem was they had to make money, particularly in the early part of the century when the internet was eating into their business. Some companies responded by being innovative about how they presented their information and others went down the celebrity exposé route. For the first few years of my career in London, exciting as it was, I sometimes wished I was back on a small paper because I felt more at ease writing about local politics than famous people."

"Why did you do it then?"

"I was getting valuable experience even if it wasn't what I wanted to do. It was my first job on a national paper and I took it to get a start, not to spend the rest of my life there. I didn't stay for very long, I had a political blog where I wrote about what I was really interested in and after a couple of years it got a following, then I had a few pieces printed in other newspapers and eventually I had enough income from that and the advertising on the blog to go freelance. Funnily enough, not long after that I met your mother. She worked for a magazine I contributed to and I met her at their Christmas party."

"Yes, yes, I've heard all this before. More about the news."

"Harsh audience this evening."

"I know ... sorry, but I really want to know."

"Ok, so in theory newspapers were supposed to keep an eye on politicians but they'd all gotten a bit close. There were enquiries, court cases and eventually a Royal Charter setting out a way that regulation could be enacted. Some screamed that three hundred years of press freedom was being thrown away but truthfully it was nowhere close to that, though it was an unusual way of trying to get them to behave more responsibly. Of course, the complainers had most to lose if their ability to invade the private lives of public figures was limited but equally the politicians knew they couldn't be too draconian and the charter was seen as a gentle way of doing things. And it would have been if it wasn't for one clause that in a time of democracy looks fine."

"What's that?"

"That a two-thirds majority in parliament was needed to change any of its terms."

"Oh."

"Exactly, oh," I said as I sat back down with my coffee. "Nobody thought any one party would get so many seats and if we were still relying on elections that might be true. However, if we're dependent, as we are, on a Central Cabinet and their puppet Parliament, changes come easily so it wasn't difficult to place legal restraints on the press in the early days. Bloggers and other independent news sources suffered most, as they often argued a more extreme viewpoint because they weren't constrained by editorial or economic issues. Once The Communication Protection Laws came in, members of the regulatory board set up under the charter disbanded themselves in protest, but this meant things only got worse as they were replaced by Central Cabinet collaborators. At that point press freedom really did end."

"They aren't the only part of the media that provide news, what about TV or radio?"

"They'd always lived under different rules because television in particular was seen as being able to influence people so had to be relatively impartial. That made it less controversial for the most part and easily cowed when new laws came in. As a much newer technology it didn't have the same historically elevated status as the press so wasn't seen as a defender of democracy even though newspapers had as much, if not more, hold on the people who read them. It was no real surprise that one of the early focuses for government control was the media in all its forms, particularly the ring-fencing of the internet and our informational division from the outside world."

"According to what we're taught in school, separating ourselves was done for our protection to stop enemies gaining access to and destroying our data systems and further strengthen us as an island nation, making decisions for its own betterment and not the benefit of others."

"You have been listening in citizenship class, haven't you? Of course it does but it also handily stops us seeing any awkward truths the government doesn't want us to know. The isolationist mentality this promotes and sustains only really became fashionable in the last couple of decades. It also ignores the existence of Northern Ireland, which continues to drift away, and the fact that Scotland voted for independence when Britain was still democratic, so the territorial claim that Britain is still an island nation is mostly for politically patriotic purposes. Those feelings had always bubbled under the surface, but mostly just in minority groups that tended to be a bit racist.

"When immigration became a dirty word during the Tory/LibDem coalition and especially in the 2015 general election battle, all the parties tried to show they were tough, so the rhetoric about how bad it was for the country became increasingly mean, even though most analyses showed there were economic benefits in allowing people from abroad to work here. The problem was that social benefits were difficult to prove because politicians and the media fed the public horror stories about immigrants abusing our benefits system or the EU allowing the country to be overrun, creating a mistrust of anyone non-British.

"As the economy deteriorated it was easy for politicians to inflate the problem for votes. Unemployment was high and wages were flat as household costs rose and the general sense was that something had to change so rather than accept publicly that any of them had anything to do with the problem or could do anything about it, politicians chose an easy scapegoat, creating a vicious circle of unpleasantness that wasn't backed up by fact."

A couple of months after that 2020 visit, the general election was cancelled and it became difficult to concentrate on the political work I'd become known for. A visit from two men who obviously weren't who they said they were not long before the suspension of democracy, to where my family were supposedly safest, undermined my confidence in what I felt was my job and made my own position feel more fragile.

At the start, it was hard to imagine the cruelty stretching outside the immigrant groups it had been designed to target. Then more warnings like the original one came with a regular update on where it was felt you had positioned yourself within what became known as The Emergency, a chilling conversation after more than twenty years of working relatively freely. As the house visits continued and the government became more resolute, it was obvious that this situation, which suited politicians more than it did people, was becoming permanent.

I was fairly certain I was being watched so bought equipment on the black market to sweep our home for bugs and began to use less electronic communications. Work, though, began to dry up as more mainstream newspapers and websites began to drop the kind of commentary that wasn't 'appreciated in the current context' as one government mouthpiece put it. In early 2022, a disparate but focussed group of us banded together to start a website, publishing our writing and continuing our questioning of emergency powers. We gathered together like-minded technicians, developers, journalists and editors into what could best be described as the communal efforts of a bunch of aging believers in democracy and press freedom. By the middle of the year, it had been blocked without explanation, though it was obvious why. We continued to try and get our message out, bouncing the server locations around, but eventually we seemed to be constantly struggling to get to a point where even a couple of people saw what we wrote.

As several of us sat around one evening in our front room, mulling over how to continue and in what form, I think we all knew that we were now considered to be on the wrong side, not much better than those that had been interred. We hadn't held back in our criticism of what we had taken to playfully calling The Regime, but in our old-fashioned way we had expected it to open up a debate about when elections might be held or when people in the camps would be put on trial. Instead the focus on us personally increased and we were all requested to come to the newly formed Ministry for Stability for an informal chat.

"If there was no real proof that it was harmful," Cassie said as she got up to go to the fridge, "how did they manage to make immigration such an issue? Didn't people see the falseness of it?"

"The gradual shift from evidence-based policy to style over substance to disregarding evidence altogether helped blinker people to truth. It was the kind of thing that accelerated under Blair and got even worse after the 2010 election. Real political debate began to disappear in a cacophony of anger and dubious interpretations of statistics. The Liberal Democrats, who were the smaller partner in government, weren't used to power and the country wasn't used to two parties ruling. A lot of policies were pushed through unhindered that just enhanced disparities that already existed, and there was a sort of crass demonization of not just immigrants but several sections of society, a tradition that continues today, but far more dangerously. That coalition, and particularly the Tories, strengthened the ideological foundations that are now used to withdraw basic services from people accused of various offences against the state."

"We were taught in Stability Economics that it's the only way to force an unproductive person to do something that benefits the country," Cassie said as she sat back down with a pot of yoghurt.

"That's a convenient way for politicians to claim a lack of responsibility for people they have no interest in. David Cameron used to talk about the idea of 'The Big Society' that would take care of people as a matter of conscience.

Nobody realised he meant referring them to food banks and homeless shelters rather than maintaining a support network. It made the degradation of a significant part of the population acceptable, allowing the media and by extension the rest of the country the freedom to consider the poor and disabled as undeserving of our help and humanity. The bad cases that were publicised were presented as evidence that everyone who claimed benefits was dishonest, conveniently ignoring the people who were genuinely unable to work or couldn't find a job because the economy was a mess. Throughout the five years of that government poverty and inequality increased massively and it made mainstream the political values that conjured images of immigrants and the poor clamouring at the door of the benefits office. The politicians that came after, who still rule today, continue to embrace that philosophy as a means to provide no safety net at all because it's easy to be blind to individual suffering when your social position means you never have to see it."

"Ok, my economics lessons just sound a bit heartless now."

"They are but that's nothing new. That national mood of intolerance meant it wasn't particularly shocking in 2015 when a relatively new party called UKIP held the balance of power after the election. They campaigned more or less totally on leaving the European Union and cutting immigration and they had, while not necessarily the outright support of the media, the advantage of having most of the mass-circulation newspapers agreeing with their pub politics. Labour and the Conservatives won about the same number of seats, but neither had the majority needed to govern. UKIP were ideologically closer to the Tories, so they formed a new coalition. The Conservatives then ditched David Cameron and chose a guy called Martin Ashbey as their new leader. He'd been skulking around the cabinet for some time, and had fairly strong views on immigration and security, so was well placed to partner UKIP even though, or possibly because, he was one of the main proponents of policies without evidence.

"Then UKIP elected Fred Ogby as their parliamentary leader and he became Deputy Prime Minister. In the couple of years before the election, they had publicly tried to weed out some of the more trenchant views of their members, but it became clear when they were in power that had all been a subterfuge to gain votes, which worked. Ogby was as extreme as you could get when it came to UKIP's core values, and Ashbey and he set about creating some of the most backward immigration legislation possible at the same time as continually purging the government of those that didn't agree with them. Their joy at being able to enact their fantasies of deportation and control was somewhat sickening to observe and a clumsy warning of what was to come.

"Then of course they started on the European Union. A few years before that election the Tories had promised a referendum on whether Britain should leave and it became a coalition condition that it happened. It was always going to be a losing battle so we announced our departure in 2017. That, it would be fair to say, was a tumultuous time."

"How come?"

"There was nothing gentle about Britain's exit even though it could have been done more tactfully. We weren't part of the Euro, so there were no currency complications but any European working here had to apply for a visa and the majority were refused. A lot of people left of their own accord as well and in the end nearly two million people returned home over the course of a year on top of the half a million or so who'd already been deported. For months bus stations, ports and airports were clogged as this enormous flow of people left, dragging whatever belongings they had behind them.

"That was around the time my parents left, even though Irish people were allowed to stay. The unnerving feeling your grandparents got watching immigrants being rounded up was stronger than I realised at the time. They'd lived here since the 1970s and put up with occasional discrimination in the early days, but to them this was different. As my father put it, 'Once they've gotten rid of the Asians, the Africans, the Americans, the Middle-Easteners, the East-Europeans and the West-Europeans they don't want, the economy may still be bolloxed and they'll need something else to divert everyone's attention. Who's to say they won't start looking at us'."

"I didn't know that was why they left. I thought they just decided it would be nice to retire back in Ireland."

"They did but the sweeping bedlam forced them into thinking about it, otherwise they might never have left the country where all their children and grandchildren live. They'd rather have stayed, but I guess they saw something that spooked them."

"I'd like to see them again one day, in person instead of on a screen."

"I hope you will."

Cassie got up, threw her yoghurt pot in the bin and stared out the kitchen window for a moment.

"So what happened next?" she said.

"Well, within a few months, nearly all British government staff had been recalled with only a trade delegation remaining who signed an agreement very early on so the flow of goods and money wouldn't be affected. But everything else was gone, any adherence to EU laws, any debate about the relationship with our neighbours, which became do it our way or we won't deal with you. I'm not saying that everything about the EU was good and it certainly needed reform, but by today's standards the majority of Britain's people would be better off inside, if only because it safeguards some rights for workers and had begun to moderate the worst excesses of the banking industry that caused the recession which led to the unemployment and despondency that allowed anti-EU and immigration feeling to take hold. That led to the next predictable step, the repeal of the Human Rights Act, even though it had nothing to do with the EU."

"We learnt about that in history, it was the act

imposed by Europe that restricted the government from ruling in Britain's interests."

"Fascinating. In reality it was a British bill that enshrined some articles of the European Convention on Human Rights in UK law. It was brought in very early in Blair's first term, one of the contradictions of Labour's tenure given their attitude to civil liberties. I think the day that act was abolished was the day I knew we were finally on a self-destructive path that I'd never be able to agree with."

"Why? What value did it add to our lives?"

"Nothing instantly recognisable but not everything needs to be used every day for it to be valuable. Some things are just good to have available should they be needed at some point. The Convention was created after World War Two to try and ensure that nothing like that could ever happen again by setting out the rights of individuals. I've told you before about the rise of Hitler, concentration camps, genocide and the outcome of the war. This document, created by the European Court of Human Rights, which almost every European country was part of, set out things like the equal rights of people regardless of ethnicity or religion, people's right to privacy and also the principles of a free press as a way of holding government to account. The symbolic act of removing elements of it from our law book signalled an end to what had been a long running debate about whether we should even be recognising it anymore. For years politicians bitched about it and at one point a sympathetic judge even suggested it was only there as a guide for the purposes of political criticism rather than anything legally binding, the kind of commentary that by definition also devalued our rights. I mean, it had often been ignored but it did at least provide some principles which if you look at it in human terms is a good start. It's in people's nature to feel injustice, but often only relative to their position in the abuse chain, so those repealing the act were never going to suffer from its demise.

"Britain eventually and unsurprisingly stated it would no longer recognise the European Court as having jurisdiction over domestic decisions, which was popular internally in that isolationist way. That alone didn't seem too sinister unless you knew the details, and most people didn't. It was just a footnote in history by that time, and people have a tendency to forget the past if they have no personal connection to it, or they at least lose sight of its contemporary context after a couple of generations. Also, some of the media played it up as a poke in the eye for Europe and reclamation of British control over its own affairs. Not many questioned the value of effectively removing an individual's access to the last possible challenge to government. Again, just like the European Union, not all its judgements were logical but as an institution it was nice to have around for our personal protection."

I got up and started clearing dishes from the table and filling the dishwasher as Cassie fidgeted with the salt cellar.

"But wasn't this just the idea that we should take back

control of our country, that we shouldn't have to answer to anyone outside our own borders?"

"It's a bit more complicated than that. From a politician's point of view, European law and the Human Rights Act had an effect on parliamentary sovereignty."

"What's that?"

"It was one of the constitutional conventions set out in the Bill of Rights that allowed Parliament to rule on behalf of the monarch so that all power wouldn't be in the hands of an individual. It still exists as the de facto way the country is run today but the theory in the past was that MPs would legislate in the interests of the people and any bills passed by Parliament would be upheld by the courts because of that. However, not just the Convention on Human Rights but European Union legislation became law meaning the government had to abide by plenty of regulations it didn't make. Some of those were good, some of them weren't as happens with any legislative body, but more importantly I think some governments, or possibly just individuals, felt they'd lost some of the ability to implement their ideologies. At the same time the last hundred years saw the loss of an empire coupled with a reduction in stature internationally, as well as the slow determined devolution of power to Northern Ireland and Wales and the independence of Scotland, so the English Parliament no longer had the power it once had over countries, regions and people.

"And that's not forgetting the judiciary. Parliament had to adjust to the fact that the courts could now rule against them because of European legislation, when historically they would only have had to interpret British law which could be created, modified or repealed by the ruling party. So when the opportunity came to regain some of the sovereignty they once exercised, politicians were quick to grasp it. Their loss of power could be seen as a factor in everything that happened after 2017, a series of declarations to disprove impotence."

"I think I'm beginning to see where this tale is going."

"Yes, but it was only after the bombings that things really accelerated, particularly in terms of how the courts worked. They were still fairish if someone was determined enough and had the cash to take their case to the highest level. The Supreme Court would interpret points of law, and it remained reasonably independent right up until the early twenties. The problem was the law gradually changed and they were powerless to stop that after the dissociation from Europe, even though centuries of traditional rights were disintegrating around them. Long before that legal aid, which allowed even the poorest person to go to court, had been cut back and then completely removed so it was no longer an option if someone felt they had been wronged by the government, essentially removing the right to a fair trial. People couldn't afford solicitors so often had to represent themselves in an area they had no experience of and the resulting convictions became difficult to appeal. Eventually the very vague terms of The Stability Laws were used to bypass courts altogether on the grounds that they sometimes delayed the implementation of security procedures.

"Once the public lost faith in them as being independent or of any use, it was easy to remove funding. Then they were privatised and had mission statements to follow and quotas to fill to keep prisons going, making them another cog in the corporate-governance world rather than upholders of what had once been the law. Now they rule on crime and occasionally rubber stamp government policy. Like every other public service, they've been ripped apart and any judges considered objectionable have been forced out or retired."

"Isn't the job of the courts to punish criminals, I don't understand what other purpose they serve? What do you mean by the Supreme Court interpreting points of law?"

"In the past the judiciary had a lot of power and like everything else, it wasn't perfect but it did act as a restraint. It prided itself on its independence because that was part of its purpose as one of the three branches of power. Courts weren't just there to throw people in jail though obviously that was a part of their job, they also interpreted the laws that parliament passed to ensure they were compatible with the rule of law. When it came down to it though, if the government chooses to ignore its rulings, it fast becomes irrelevant."

"What are the three branches of power?"

"Government, Parliament and the courts, sometimes called the executive, legislature and judiciary, each of which should be independent of the other. The theory is that if you have separate bodies with a certain level of power that the other branches depend on, you avoid a descent into dictatorship as one branch can always overrule the other. There was some reform during the Labour years which separated the judiciary further from politicians but that all seems unimportant now."

"All those bodies still exist though, why doesn't it work anymore?"

"Again, there's an element of goodwill needed which is now missing, plus the fact that military and security strength lies with The Central Cabinet, who are still the equivalent of the executive, but the other branches have lost their power. Theoretically of course, the king rules over all of them as head of state."

"So why doesn't he do anything?"

"Good question. The position of the Royal Family is a little difficult to work out because they don't speak about it as they aren't constitutionally allowed to become involved in the day-to-day running of the country."

"I understand that but surely they have some moral obligation to us, their subjects?"

"Perhaps, but they can't really interfere in the workings of Parliament and by extension The Central Cabinet because the parts of the Bill of Rights that deal with that kind of thing were written into The Stability Laws. Now, nobody really knows what's said in Ashbey's weekly meetings at the palace but the king can't just come out in public and criticise what's happening, whether he might want to personally or not. It's the main reason William is on the throne and not his father, because Charles used to write to MPs on a regular basis to try and get them to take up causes he had an interest in, which caused a minor constitutional crisis because it was seen as a monarch interfering with the workings of Parliament."

"Wouldn't that kind of intervention now be in the best interests of the people being ruled?"

"Maybe but we're talking about constitutional realities, such as they are, not morality. What you have to remember, aside from all the historical stuff, is that the ability to vote in elections, the checks and balances on government or the right to a fair trial were never functions of the monarchy, those things were granted by politicians, and taken away just as easily."

"Ok, but the royals are in the news all the time, visiting charities or whatever. They look like they care so why are they ignoring the abuses of those same people."

"Well, who's to say they're not in the same position as everyone else, afraid to speak out. Of course, the more cynical among us would say that they're also dependent on the state for money. They get a grant every year and like councils may have been threatened with removal of funds if they didn't keep quiet. Nobody really knows the truth but you are right, they don't say much about it. The other issue of course is that officially the monarch is head of the armed forces as well so in theory the military serve the crown, but in reality The Central Cabinet dictate their operations as well."

"So William couldn't just order the army to take over and restore democracy?"

"I suppose he could but there are plenty of officers

with a vested interest in keeping the status quo. Without a real police force, they get a lot more money for defence of the nation, which involves less fighting abroad now and more guarding the country internally. In terms of their loyalty to the monarch, it may be that they believe they are protecting the crown in the same way as the security service, in order to stop the country being overrun in this supposed war."

"Doesn't anyone in the military care that they're involved in hurting their own people? They must have families too."

"The defence minister's deputies are the heads of the army, navy and air force so the state itself is militarised. Most soldiers are just following orders and are posted a distance away from their home towns to get around the possibility of them having to deal with family and friends. People sign up because it's a good job with decent enough wages and a supposedly secure future. They're trained to take part in wars but are being deployed to one in their own country even though the majority just sit in base waiting for something to happen."

"That doesn't sound very true to the Stability Economics theories of productivity, efficiency and cost-cutting."

"It's not but The Central Cabinet need their presence as a deterrent. They're seen now and again just to show people that even though the police and their helpers can handle most of the cruelty, should there be a need for more the army can be called, while the rest of the armed forces patrol our borders to make sure nobody can sneak in or out with ideas that might harm Stability.

I almost used to prefer when they were abroad playing bit parts in questionable wars than their current role of chief isolationist force. Their only international roles now are the occasional drone attacks in Scotland or Ireland targeting opposition exiles, and of course their consultancy services."

"What are those?"

"Our military is still respected internationally and has always been good at inventing new technology, so they sell their services as mercenary forces in faraway places. It allows other countries to make payments to Britain that appear to be related to training or equipment but in fact involve running unaccountable clandestine killings. It's sanctioned by the government because outsourcing brings in money and the few operations they can openly talk about allow them to claim some part in the international fight against terrorism, which fits nicely with the propaganda campaign here."

I have no idea who spoke to me that day in the ministry. There was a constant, unidentifiable flow of bureaucracy from ten in the morning until four that afternoon. I was interviewed at length about my intentions towards the government, as if I was about to enter into a life-long union with them. The method of questioning was meant to disorientate and it had that effect, keeping me guessing as to what they wanted.

As the day went on I realised they were judging my strengths and weaknesses, whether it might be possible to influence me in some way. Just before I was allowed to leave, they made their sales pitch. I was to stop writing critical articles or there would be consequences, which they laid out very clearly.

"Mr. O'Dwyer, do you love your family?" said the latest apparatchik, a thin mousey-haired man with spectacles.

"I beg your pardon," I said.

"I ask only because I'm sure they would miss you, and you them."

"I don't follow. I think you should get to the point if you're trying to threaten me."

"We're not in the business of making threats Mr. O'Dwyer, I'm merely giving you some advice for your own good and that of your family."

"Go on."

"I think you know that we're a little discontented with the behaviour exhibited by you and your activist colleagues, and the effect your work is having on the stability of the country. We called you here today to try and impress on you the severity of these disruptions and their unpatriotic nature."

"That depends on your viewpoint, a desire for the restoration of democracy would seem to me to be as patriotic as you can get if you judge a country to be made up of the citizens that

live in it. I'd also question your use of the word activist. I'm a journalist. It's my job to inform people about the reality of the government's actions."

"That's all very well, but as you say it depends on your viewpoint. *The opinion of this government is that your writing could contribute to a breakdown of social order if you continue to disseminate the type of information you have been. As you're well aware the law allows us to detain those that we consider a threat to the fabric of the nation."*

"Are you saying you're going to start sending journalists to the camps?"

"I'm saying that the stability and security of the country are our prime concern, and should you wish to assist with that, we would be happy to have you on board. However, if you continue denigrating government policies in order to maintain your reputation as a political commentator, causing immeasurable damage to the strength of our society, then we may be forced to intervene. You are currently graded as a Category-3 enemy of the state under the terms of The Stability Laws. If you advance to Category-1, we would be unequivocal in our response."

I stared back at him.

"And what exactly would I have to do to advance, as you put it?"

"The processes in place to determine categorisations are confidential."

"What's the lowest level?"

"Category-5, but you will never be able to reach that due to the severity of your previous activities."

"So no matter what I do, the state has declared me an enemy for life."

"Correct."

"So it will always consider itself at war with me."

"That's one way of putting it but those aren't the terms we prefer."

"How would you put it then?"

"The guidance documentation states that a Category-3 enemy has a capacity to enter into open conflict with the state and should be loosely monitored. If unable to adapt to Stability, the subject should be reclassified as Category-2 and overseen at a personal level."

"What does that mean?"

"It would require the wearing of a location expression device at all times and a boundary system to compliment the life of the subject."

"I suppose I should be grateful it's just intimidation at the moment."

"As I said before, I am merely stating the case for your cooperation. You are free to do as you please, but think of this as a gentle reminder of the conduct we favour."

"There's fuck all gentle about what you just implied."

"There's no need for that tone Mr. O'Dwyer."

"Fine, so what happens now?"

"You are free to go."

His use of the word free seemed farcical during the last half of 2022, as the home visits became more regular and the questions more ridiculous. It was obvious they would probably go through with their threat but it still seemed surreal that they would jail journalists for disagreeing with them.

I kept the true nature of that day's conversation from Jane for some time, though it wasn't hard for her to see that something in me had changed. The new frequency of the visitations were taking their toll on all of us, particularly Cassie who became scared of any knock on the door, fearing the dour men who insisted on coming inside.

I stopped writing critical political pieces, taking work copywriting or in uncontroversial magazines. Like many of my colleagues who had been called to the ministry, I did whatever would pay the bills. This didn't stop the interrogations though, particularly when articles appeared on unblocked websites calling for revolution or laying out the latest disappearances.

I began to realise that this treatment wasn't going to stop. I was marked as the enemy, and regardless of whether I kept my head down they would keep reminding me of the fact that they had the power.

The pressure on my family was too much. Jane didn't have to operate under the same restrictions so could continue to work as she had before. The economy had been bobbing up and down for years and had become secondary to survival for most people, so the government weren't interested in what she reported for now. It was those of us who had always had a political slant that were to be watched so we wouldn't point out the underhandedness of the regime.

I can't even remember now how the conversation came about, I think Jane started it, and regrettably everything she said made sense. Early in 2023 I moved to a three-bed end terrace house a couple of streets away. I could see Cassie as much as I wanted, Jane was clear about that, almost insistent, but the negative effect the visiting officials were having on her was too much. If there had been some end in sight, it might have been different, but that wasn't the case.

Cassie and I sat scanning the papers one Sunday afternoon when she said, "Tell me about the bombings."

"Hmm, arguably that's when things really started to go bad," I said.

"I don't remember much about it."

"That's not surprising, you were only five."

"So what happened?"

"On the 21st of July, 2018, there was a series of explosions across the country, all coordinated to happen around the same time. The scale of it was the most shocking, hitting fourteen city centres from Leeds to London and Brighton to Bristol. Nearly four hundred people died and three times that were injured. Over that summer, there were sporadic bombings across the country, never as lethal as that first day, but still damaging as they moved on to data, power, transport and shipping, crippling infrastructure rather than people.

"The thing was, nobody claimed responsibility, but the nation assumed Islamic terrorists were responsible as witness statements dribbled out. Now, don't misunderstand me, it was and it appeared they'd been planning these attacks for close to a decade, but the over-exuberance of the internet created a spiral of claustrophobic fear. As with anything like this, it's always a minority of people who believe so deeply in a cause they are willing to kill and die for it. If it was a majority of the two million or so Muslims living here, then we'd have had war on the streets on a daily basis. However, the atmosphere fitted with the coalition's habit of demonizing immigrants, no matter how long they'd lived here, so they allowed speculation to take over from fact for a few days.

"Obviously a huge defence operation began as well as an investigation into how something like this could have happened. The security services were caught off guard because they'd become dependent on technology to do their jobs. The bombers, who had a tight support network, appeared to never slip up by using electronic communications. Everything was done face to face and because it happened over such a long period they were able to hide the fact that small amounts of money were constantly coming into the country and bomb-making materials were gradually being stockpiled, bypassing normal monitoring processes. Depressingly, the people who missed it only gained more power as they said they'd need to expand their operations to counter the increased threat. That was the thing, the media, as they often did at the time, grabbed at the wrong part of the story, questioning first why they hadn't stopped it, then when they said they needed more resources, supporting the propping up of a failed system rather than focussing on why whoever had done it felt justified in causing such a great loss of life."

"But surely finding out why it was allowed to happen was more important."

"Actually, I don't agree, but I'm in the minority. When within the last thirty years the country has been involved in two wars that have failed to improve the lives of people in the invaded countries, it would be better to look at the longer term effects of pissing off whole populations with an arrogant foreign policy than obsessing about an internal problem like the impossibility of watching everyone. For years this whole issue has been called The War on Terror, when really it wasn't a war at all, more of a long-running ideological clash which existed way before the turn of the century. The problem was that Tony Blair and George Bush, the US president at the time of the New York attacks, emphasised the religious aspect of this hypothetical war, as the declared enemy were Muslims. Bush even said that God told him to invade Iraq and the two of them prayed together as they were planning it. As with all religions, you shouldn't group everyone who believes in it into one easily criticised group because that just creates resentment, but it's easier for governments to do that, particularly when it suits some other purpose."

"Like what?"

"Like the creation of fear. Britain and the US used the convenient horror of terrorism to try and convince people the invasion of Iraq was necessary, as well as the kidnap and torture programs and the later drone campaigns. Donald Rumsfeld, the US defence secretary at the time even went as far as making ludicrous statements about having to shackle and hood prisoners as they were being transported because they might chew through cables on planes to crash them."

"Huh?"

"I know, but that kind of outlandish statement became normal and fed into the fear creation industry that helped rally support, particularly in the US. Years later several soldiers who'd been involved spoke out and questioned why they had been there at all. They thought they were freedom fighters when they were just pawns in some personal game being played out by their political masters in pursuit of ideology, oil and defence contracts. Interestingly Rumsfeld was also involved in exaggerating the threat from the Soviet Union during the Cold War."

"Sounds like a great person to have around in a crisis."

"Indeed, but after the bombings the government here used the same tactics, encouraging, or at least allowing, the development of an atmosphere whereby most of the public became nervous of anybody Asian, African or Middle-Eastern looking. In fairness the kind of racial profiling that views every dark-skinned person as a potential terrorist had been practiced by the police and border control agency for years so it wasn't difficult for people on the streets to follow what looked like officially sanctioned policy. Vigilante groups grew up around the country to monitor their neighbours, reporting anything they considered unusual to the authorities and sometimes acting on their suspicions. Innocent people were attacked and murdered simply because of the colour of their skin, and many mosques and businesses were burnt to the ground. Rather than condemn this barbarous ignorance, the government produced guidelines that suggested ways in which their non-British neighbours could be watched, which included a few half-hearted lines about not taking the law into your own hands. Without the restrictions of any internationally recognised human rights convention, they could do as they pleased. Anyone who tried to take them to the European Court, which was still legally an option but mostly symbolic, found they were at best harassed, at worst deported."

"Wasn't all of this necessary during The Emergency? Aside from perhaps the vigilante groups, didn't the authorities need to make a strong statement about security?"

"That may be what you're taught now, but the victimisation of whole cultures or nationalities because of the actions of a minority isn't right, whether you agree with their values or not. The bombings were appalling and should never have happened but as a country we misplaced our decency when we decided to lock up anyone who might once have had a thought, made a youthful mistake or was just related to someone. Also, it wasn't called The Emergency at first, that's just one of the many PR rewrites of history. It was a set of existing laws that already allowed the government to detain those suspected of terrorist offences without access to lawyers, or a trial for that matter. Public opinion was so polarised that no political party would speak up against their expansion to include not just electronic tagging of suspected terrorists but their internment and the registration of everyone who attended a mosque, making people nervous about practising their religion, another freedom that went with the Human Rights Act. Some individual politicians, journalists and human rights organisations did speak out, but they were drowned out by hysteria. Soon after, the camps were set up on military bases around the country and The Sympathiser Laws a few months later allowed the detention of friends and families of suspects at the discretion of the authorities. So it became legal for the government to inter people without trial, purely for being associated with someone who was suspected of being involved in terrorism."

"That's what happened to Iqbal and his family, isn't it?"

"Yeah, that's how misused those laws became and it's also a good point about the religious side of things. His family were never involved in anything but happened to be Muslim. They'd been here since the 1950s so Iqbal was the fourth generation to grow up here and they'd all made a life for themselves without ever being a burden on the state. It wasn't until after his cousin had been shipped off in early 2025 after a tip-off to the police that they rounded up the rest of the extended family using surveillance and brute force. It seems unlikely any of them were involved in anything, given they'd managed to survive seven years of emergency powers and vigilantism without any harm for no other reason than they were respected and liked by the community they lived in. I heard his cousin got on the wrong side of someone in a street argument when they told him to go back to Terrorland or wherever it was he came from and the next day the police picked him up."

"That's how it works now, you only have to come from the wrong country, or have the wrong face, and you're considered guilty on the basis of anonymous information. I mean, he's in his twenties so might have some chance of dealing rationally with the injustice. I can't see how imprisoning Iqbal when he's twelve is going to lead to long term stability. He was born and raised here but the country turned against him in pursuit of some supposedly greater ideal, which I'm still having trouble seeing. It's difficult to imagine him or any of his family ever having warm feelings for Britain again. The abuse of innocent people does not make them cherish the bond they might otherwise have with their country. They're more likely to feel anger, if not hatred, for the UK and that isn't going to be good for our much advertised security."

"Why does the government do it, why be so cruel if it's not going to improve anything?"

"Because they think they're right I suppose, I don't really know. It's become a secretive affair where people just disappear, and no amount of questioning of the authorities will reveal their whereabouts. It's as if they've been plucked from life by a stealthy beast. Emergency laws had been in place for a few years when Iqbal and his family vanished and over that time, the Ministry for Stability have perfected their techniques and entrenched the security surrounding the internment camps. You can't get anywhere near them or find out what happens there anymore. Every now and then, somebody will release a few pictures they've managed to sneak but they're rarely seen. That would be contrary to national security apparently."

"Have you seen any of them?"

"Yes, printed copies often do the rounds of interested journalists and are destroyed before the security service get to them."

"Do you see the people who are being held?"

"Yes sweetie, but I've never seen Iqbal or any of his family. I'm sorry."

"What do you see then?"

"It's not pleasant Cassie."

"I want to know."

I looked at her, trying to gauge in her concerned face how much detail I should tell her.

"The pictures I've seen are of listless and bewildered people who look like they've lost the will to live," I said. "I can't describe it any other way. They look like the stresses of being imprisoned are dragging them down. That was the strangest thing about the photos back in the early twenties, their clothes often came from charities and they were allowed freedom under surveillance within the confines of their camp so they looked healthy enough, but like they're still wondering what they'd done. The most recent images I saw were taken in 2027 and bravely that photographer managed to release the images abroad. Not long after she wasn't heard from again, but whether she's disappeared or gone into exile I don't know. Those were the most shocking images I'd seen since all this began, and it makes it worse when you realise it's only a hundred miles from here."

"What was so bad about them? What happened when they were seen abroad?"

"They had unsettling similarities with photos from Second World War concentration camps, and most European countries were quick to point that out. The clothes of the detainees had become more ragged and they didn't look as well fed as they had before. In some ways that was around the time our transition to tyranny was complete, when it was clear the state had finally extinguished any guilt about its human rights abuses. The camps were in the hands of private contractors and the government openly said conditions weren't their fault because a set fee had been paid for their operation which was sufficient to cover all necessary expenses.

"The interesting thing is, the rest of Europe tightened up their human rights legislation and strengthened civil liberties, so maybe our excesses have done some good in other countries. Of course almost nobody in Britain saw the pictures and the government had stopped caring what the outside world thought. It was only a few years ago and nearly a decade of slowly but surely squeezing the fight out of people who would once have been enraged meant they could stamp out access to the pictures and conversation about them pretty quickly."

"Dad, do you think Iqbal and his family could be dead?"

"I can't say sweetie. Look, the likelihood is they're alive. I know I said the camps had become extremely secretive and the photos were shocking but I do sometimes hear snippets from sources that I don't dare publish. Some of the camps are fine, they're still prisons where people are held without any regard to their rights, but they are at least feeding them something. That much we know. In the first few years, the stories that came out were pretty shocking. All the torture techniques that had been perfected during the wars in Afghanistan and Iraq were resurrected in the high security camps where they sent those they felt were most dangerous, not the families. Waterboarding, sleep deprivation and what can only be described as fairly rough questioning were all used after the bombings to extract dubious confessions. What was happening was bad enough that many soldiers broke ranks and became whistleblowers. Almost every journalist had their own contact in the camps for a while and stories were printed constantly for a couple of years before the government began to silence the media and secure the camps."

"How do you know these things? I mean, not the things from years ago, the more recent stuff. How do you find it all out?"

"I'm a journalist, and was for twenty years before any of this happened. Whether I write or publish any of this I still try to keep track of what's going on, because someday I hope I'll be able to write it down so future generations can look back and see it was the wrong thing to do."

After moving out, my visits from the government settled into a quarterly pattern, where I was asked about my recent activities and any undesirably public statements I had made were pointed out. Perhaps because they could no longer terrorise my family at the same time it became more routine and less intimidating, or they knew they had the upper hand as my work was far less controversial.

In early 2025, somehow stories began to leak from the camps again, describing how primitive conditions were becoming. The drive to 'increase efficiencies within the detention market' seemed to be nothing more than cutting out the nutritional value of prisoners' meals and, in a masterful accounting move, extending the supposed life expectancy of clothing and bedding so it wouldn't be necessary to buy new ones for a few more years, leaving prisoners in rags and sleeping in increasingly decaying beds. Internees were rumoured to be locked up for most of the day and night, monitored by a new surveillance system that automatically tracked unusual behaviour inside the sixty-four-person bunkhouses that accommodated everyone, handily cutting the number of staff needed. The inhumanity was clear to some, and talked about in hushed tones between good friends for a while before a number of strikes broke out in support of the prisoners.

The government feared these locally-based rebellions would spread and ultimately lead to open revolt against them, not just employers. A show of force from the newly-privatised police force broke up most of the pickets but while they were occupied the hacking and bombing started and it became clear that this was a coordinated insurgency. Communication networks were taken down, if only for a while, and several police stations were burnt to the ground before extra soldiers were deployed to maintain order on the streets. Finally the security service mopped up by searching out anyone who may have been involved. About thirty protestors died during the couple of months of the uprising, mostly as a result of torture and beatings, but it spread no further than a few flashpoints and the state quickly regained control.

The scale, however small, spooked The Central Cabinet and once they'd finished rounding up known ringleaders and those they strongly suspected of involvement, they targeted anyone who had once objected.

In the spring of 2025 I was taken from my home for the first time, something I suppose I'd always expected at some point. I wasn't the only one – they made a point of talking to everyone on their suspicious persons list. I don't know if they continued to interrogate us because of our past indiscretions or because they actually thought we were involved, I suspect a bit of both. Mostly, I think they just wanted to show their power.

All of us who still dared speak to one other had noticed that the questioning had become more inept in the last year or so, since the home visits had been taken over by a private security firm called Stability Interrogation Services, whose staff seemed to be mostly interested in filling out a form proving they'd done their jobs. The people who came were less assured, like they'd been on a one-day training course that emphasised their representation of the company rather than the task of interrogating. The accusatory manner that always assumed something was still there but for the most part all that was needed was a strong, confident rebuttal. They would then leave with a standard warning to keep out of trouble, like I was an errant teenager who'd been caught drinking underage.

That changed the day I was abducted. They came early while I was still making coffee. I opened the door to find not just the usual bland interrogators but another four men in a familiar-looking uniform. They were the new Security Enhancement Service, or SES, another set of private contractors who had just been hired to 'aid the government in the provision of Stability' as the papers put it.

I was told I'd have to accompany them and it was then I noticed the waiting van. It was one of those blocky prisoner transporters I'd often seen on television, usually arriving at or leaving a courthouse and occasionally being attacked by an angry mob. I asked if I could get dressed first but that didn't seem to be on their list of processes for the morning.

It's odd to find yourself inside something that's so familiar from the outside. I'd always thought there was a window so prisoners had some light. Maybe there had been in the past but this one didn't, the mini-cell having just a small harsh bulb.

We bounced along for some time, and I initially tried to judge where we were going by reading the twists and turns, but eventually gave up. By the time we stopped I was disoriented, tired and not particularly quarrelsome so the dark cloth bag placed over my head and the handcuffs clicked on my wrists seemed unnecessary. My feet crunched on gravel and I could hear birds and smell lavender, none of which gave any clues as to where I was.

Inside, the bag was removed and I was in a windowless room, face to face with the thin man who had worried about the welfare of my family a few years previously. Pressure does funny things to the mind – my first thought was about the level of customer service the security service had put in place to be able to guarantee the same person would handle your interrogation over the years.

"Still fighting the good fight?" I said, noticing he seemed to have aged more than he should have.

"Mr. O'Dwyer, I think it would be best if you didn't make jokes."

"Really, six men to collect a moderately unfit forty-five-year-old from his house before he's even had a chance to get dressed. I'd say there has to be a joke in there somewhere."

"I really would suggest you limit your talking to answering my questions."

"Thanks for the advice."

"So, let's begin," he said, officiously swiping a tablet in front of him.

"Mr. O'Dwyer, are you a member of The Activists?"

"What, no foreplay?" I said to what can best be described as a withered, exasperated look. "As I've said many times before to those miserable arseholes who intrude on my life, no, I am not a member of a fictitious group created by the government to justify keeping certain sections of the population in check."

"Mr. O'Dwyer, I suggest you lose the sarcasm. You are in a place where no one will find you, where you can disappear if we choose."

"So you expect me to answer your questions dishonestly then?"

"No, I expect you to keep to the facts and not embellish your answers with irrelevant opinion."

"I see."

And I did. This wasn't the same person who had interviewed me a few years previously. Something had hardened and what manufactured friendliness there had been was gone. Perhaps he had failed to get a promotion and was resentful of his employers, or worse, he did and this was the result.

"I hope you do," he said, tapping the tablet once to record my answer, *"because The Central Cabinet has grown tired of constant attacks that seek to undermine the durability of the state. We no longer believe these are the random acts of crazed individuals. The Activists, according to the intelligence we have, are now a more organised, focussed group who are intent on bringing down the government."*

"And you believe I have something to do with this?"

"You are from an older time, one that is no longer relevant, and the beliefs you expressed during the winding down of the previous system are contrary to the stability of the state. Am I to believe that your thought processes have changed? The research the government has carried out shows that without intensive personal therapy, a subject is unlikely to modify their opinions, and even then may retain some of their previous intellectual methodology, particularly as late in life as you are."

I sat back, barely comprehending what I was hearing.

"Are you sending me for intensive personal therapy, whatever that is, or destruction, late in life as I am?"

"Destruction? I think that's a term imagined solely by you. We just want to ensure you are complying with the requests we make of you."

"So, you have no evidence that I have anything to do with

anything that's happened or The Activists, as you call them. You just dragged me from my home, locked me in a mobile cell and placed a bag over my head in the interests of compliance."

"Yes. I think what you may be failing to understand is that we are at a significant milestone in the development of the state, and the recent upsurge in unwanted events has forced us to tighten the processes by which we protect our stakeholders."

"What is this milestone?"

"That is a matter for the government but it is no secret that administrative functions will soon be re-launched following a period of reappraisal, and if you don't mind I'll ask the questions."

"Sorry, once a journalist and all that."

"That is exactly what concerns us Mr. O'Dwyer."

"I don't follow."

"The facts are that you have in the past been a vocal critic of the work that has been carried out by The Central Cabinet, whose efforts have led to a stability that benefits the nation in immeasurable ways. What we are concerned about is that you may still harbour some resentment about the fact that you were wrong and seek to participate in activities that may impact on the permanence of the state. Your comments during the regular sit-downs with our internal ambassadors betray your feelings about the efficacy of the processes put in place."

"You say it as if I take part in those little meetings in my living room willingly."

"That is not on my list of issues for discussion. We are concerned that you do not believe fully in the protective re-organisation of our society, that while you may not currently

be a member of The Activists, you do sympathise with them and harbour some Activist-like thoughts. It has always been clear to us that, regardless of its worryingly undefined hierarchy, you carried out a management role in the protest movement during the early part of this decade."

"I'd have to say firstly that you don't really know my thoughts. Thankfully you haven't yet gotten inside the minds of people. All you're trying to get from me is a dull declaration for the sake of the camera behind you. That recording will then be filed away until the next time, when a new recording will be made to be filed with the first one, and so on so that in the unlikely event that anyone checks, I have had my interrogation, and what I presume are the processes of control have been completed. Above all, the virtual box will have been ticked. So, again for the camera, I would like to say that I am not a member of The Activists, nor have I ever been, and I do not sympathise with them or harbour any Activist thoughts. Nor was I ever in a management role as you so anally put it, we were a group of writers who, as you well know, didn't agree with the way the country was going. Protesting was a right we used to have, in case you'd forgotten."

"Thank you Mr. O'Dwyer," he said, seemingly happy as he tapped and swiped at his tablet. "That brings me to this."

He pushed a printed sheet of paper across at me and said, "Is this your work?"

I looked at the words on the page and had to admit there was something familiar about what I was reading but answered no.

"We're not so sure," he said, "software analysis of your political articles from the time before Stability show remarkable similarities with the style and content of this piece. It was written six weeks ago and posted on a government website as part of the recent attacks."

"I think you know the things I've written recently are a little less serious than this."

"That wasn't the question I asked. Our software has flagged this up as ninety per cent certain to have been written by you."

"Perhaps you should focus on the ten per cent uncertainty then because it's not my work."

"I would be more interested in how you would explain the ninety per cent."

"Ok, software is only as good as the people who write it, and there are not too many guarantees that it gets everything right, particularly with the kind of subjective analysis that should probably be done by humans. Also, just because something is similar to what I used to write a few years ago does not necessarily mean it was written by me. Someone could be copying my style to cover their tracks or has been moved by my past work. Who knows?"

"We have every faith in the accuracy of our software and consider a ninety per cent positive match to be within the tolerances set out in the specification documentation, so I'm afraid we aren't particularly open to that sphere of argument. As for your assertion that someone may have been inspired by your past work, the processes in place to maintain non-distribution of your more harmful words are impenetrable, so I'm afraid we can't see that being a factor either."

I stared at him, momentarily gathering my thoughts while I tried to interpret the logic that had led them to me that morning.

"So you have judged me guilty without any evidence, based on the analysis of a piece of software."

"This meeting is not about the allocation of blame, it's about safeguarding the risks to our stakeholders."

There was nothing more I could think of to say. I shrugged my shoulders.

"Mr. O'Dwyer, this is the end of our conversation today, but for some reason I suspect I'll be seeing you again," he said, tapping out a pattern on the tablet.

"I'm increasing the occurrence of your sit-downs, though obviously we can't guarantee the time or day they'll occur, nor can I tell you what the new frequency will be," he said, with all the charm of a call centre organising the delivery of a new washing machine.

With that he gathered his things and left the room before the four horsemen of the SES returned, reversing the process that had brought me there.

Cassie and I sat at the kitchen table a couple of weeks later leafing through university prospectuses when she said, "Was the cancellation of elections a big surprise?"

"Yes and no, if we'd all stopped to think about it, probably not, but people were just getting on with their lives, trying to regain ordinariness after the bombings. From a political viewpoint things never really went back to normal – the harsher language from government, the emphasis on securing prosperity, public suggestions that journalists should refrain from criticism, human rights organisations accused of supporting terrorism, the restrictions placed on information as well as the cancelling of elections – so much happened in the four years between the bombings and what The Central Cabinet called the reinvigoration of the legal framework in 2022. All the decrees released that year – Stability, Communication Protection, Education, the new constitution – each one of them wrote into law the extra restrictions that had gradually encroached on our lives since the bombings yet gave expansive freedoms to our rulers and employers. The thing was, all or even some of this should have been the cue for revolution, but it just didn't happen."

"Why not, aside from the fact that it would threaten stability of course?"

"You have to look at the wider picture. By 2018 the economy was still struggling and a lower standard of living had become a fact of life for many people. Leaving the EU provided a temporary lift as Britain cut away much of the regulation companies had to abide by in other parts of Europe, though it's questionable whether that improved anybody's lives. It was good for business and it did mean more jobs, but companies could dictate their terms and that meant lower pay and fewer rights for workers so overall nothing much changed for the average person.

"After the bombings, firms began to question whether it was still a good idea to operate in a country that might not be as secure as they would have liked. Some of the targets that summer were commercial so there was a bit of disruption to communication and supply lines. This forced the government to act by bringing the military out to protect strategic locations so, superficially at least, they showed industry they were willing to do whatever it took to protect trade.

"This was long before the SES existed so to convince the general public this was the best way of protecting the country they had to use different tactics, like asking why anyone would question the moral correctness of what they did in the interests of national prosperity. By repeating messages like that over and over again, they were able to convince a majority of the population that harsh measures were needed to preserve the British way of life and in particular the economy. By the time elections were cancelled, they'd more or less won that propaganda battle."

"But what about Parliament? If it really had the power to hold the executive to account, why didn't it? Why didn't opposition politicians say something?"

"Ah, yes. That was their genius play as it happened.

The announcement about the elections happened in April, but for several weeks before that, the cabinet and their equivalent opposites in what was called the shadow cabinet had held secret talks where they agreed to share government rather than go into conflict against the national interest. You have to understand that over the years politics had become more of a job than a vocation. The view of many people was that they were in it for themselves rather than the country and voter apathy was endemic. Sometimes there were electoral surprises and protest votes but for the most part, being an MP was a long term career and the benefits were good, so when it came to cancelling elections, they were so eager not to lose out that even after decades of animosity, sharing undeserved power with their foes was more attractive than putting their futures in the hands of the people."

"You mean all this happened because they wanted to keep their jobs?"

"That might be cynical and simplistic and of course wouldn't have been the view of every politician, but it certainly was of those at the top of Labour, the Conservatives and UKIP because they made a deal they claimed was in the national interest but was really self-serving. It was only the Liberal Democrats that actually kicked up a fuss as after being routed in the 2015 election, the few MPs they had left returned to their traditional positions as rights-oriented, but they'd long since lost public trust. The day the election was cancelled the parties began the process of drafting a declaration of responsibilities, essentially carving up the available jobs between them. The statement they produced laid out vaguely how they would work together for the good of the country and handed complete control under emergency powers to the cross-party cabinet whose members were limited to the Conservatives, Labour and UKIP with Ashbey and Ogby retaining the top two jobs."

"There was dissent to begin with, and all the parties had meetings to discuss how this could possibly work, which seemed to diffuse a lot of the anger about what was effectively a coup by about fifty MPs. I heard through some contacts that once the security case was put forward and the possibility emerged that there would still be jobs going for those that kept the party line until elections were reinstated, most doubting backbench MPs changed their minds. They're still theoretically allowed to debate any issue they want but members of The Central Cabinet never go to Parliament anymore because they make all the decisions behind closed doors, so it's powerless."

"We're told in school that it's an important part of how our system works, where ideas for improving the country are put forward for consideration."

"That may very well have some truth, but for the most part it's just for show, a front to make it look like there's debate. It used to be that new bills would have several readings, be analysed, go to the House of Lords, be amended and sent back to Parliament before they could ever become law, whereas now The Central Cabinet release decrees. The power of both chambers has been stripped away or ignored, making them no more than ceremonial theme parks where tourists come to see the historical workings of parliamentary protocol. MPs are chosen from the ranks of the parties and dropped in to rule over constituencies, and they will always be people who go along with the government. This system has been going for ten years now and it's been fine tuned to keep the people who started it in power, so internal disagreement is almost non-existent."

"I'm still a bit surprised that people just accepted this."

"They'd either stopped caring or were distracted by other things. When the two main parties became increasingly similar in ideology in the late 1990s, it alienated some people as they felt there was nobody to vote for that represented them anymore. Often they just chose the party that said it was closest to their beliefs or voted strategically, whether they felt comfortable about it or not, and some people just voted for a party because that's what their family had always done. Now, that was pretty much how it had been for decades, but when people had the option, there was always the hope that they might wake from their slumber and vote more radically."

"That never happened?"

"It did, but unfortunately just to vote UKIP into power. Also, don't forget that twenty-five per cent of councils are still elected so on a local level people feel they have some say, even though it makes no real difference and was mostly used to weed out dissenting voices.

Sometimes people don't look past their neighbourhood when thinking about problems as they can see changes more easily. Whether their bins are collected or a troublesome neighbour is being dealt with are issues people will consider as important as whether the national government are working in their interests or not. I'm not saying it keeps everyone happy but it's like a consolation prize for the removal of democracy. Councils, though, were hobbled by massive funding cuts during the early part of the downturn and again in the early twenties so they can't do much apart from struggle to keep services going now. They can apply for additional funding but whether they get it or not is dependent on them allowing other things to happen."

"Like what?"

"Like surveillance or carrying out projects that make The Central Cabinet look better. The beautification of our high street only happened because of the compliance of local politicians, for which they got bonus funding for other things. Some rebelled in the early days, refusing to recognise the powers of the new national body, so the government brought in the Council Cooperation Laws in 2021, which created the 25/75 split between elected and appointed and effectively said do what we say or we cut off your money supply."

"So dissent was stamped out by threats?"

"There's still resistance, it's just more subtle and doesn't come from anywhere within the system anymore."

"The Activists?"

"They do teach you well in school don't they? What

the government call The Activists are just people that don't agree with them. It's only in the last twenty to thirty years that the word activist has become negative. There have always been people who protest about issues, whether it's a small local matter, national or international. Allowing that is something a healthy democracy should permit and accept but was one of the first things to be gradually pressured out, long before emergency powers all but outlawed it."

"What do you mean? Protesting wasn't allowed even before Stability?"

"It was but sometimes only under very limiting circumstances. It wasn't just Britain, a lot of democratic countries seemed to get sick of dealing with protestors and began to restrict them, whether it was requiring permission for a public gathering or keeping it to certain areas that neutralised the effects. Britain had its own methods which didn't wholly rely on laws. When large demonstrations were planned there were often quite gentle agreements between police and protesters about the route and estimates of how many people would turn up. Of course that didn't always work as it's difficult to control thousands of people so if anyone stepped out of line, or often even if they didn't, the police had a bunch of quite suspect methods for keeping them contained, like harassing people in the hope they didn't know their rights by using stop and search powers, dispersal laws or mass arrests. A thing called kettling was also a favourite for a while. They corralled protestors like battery chickens for hours so they couldn't go anywhere. The problem was some people got angry at being effectively imprisoned and not allowed to even go to the toilet. Eventually frustrations would boil over and somebody would try to break out, occasionally violently, which just caused the police to act the same way.

"From a legislative point of view, Blair's government outlawed protesting near The Houses of Parliament, supposedly for security reasons, which just enhanced the impression of a powerful elite keeping ordinary people at arm's length from where they ran the country and was an early step in the formal banning of legitimate protest."

"I'm not sure anyone knows what that means anymore."

"I'm pretty sure they don't. That law was made a mockery of though. There was one guy who lived outside in the street for years protesting about the UK's foreign policy. He considered he was protecting his children's future and stayed there almost until the day he died. Whenever he was arrested he went back to his place in Parliament Square and eventually they just left him there, a gentle reminder that not all protest can be pushed out of sight."

"That definitely wouldn't happen now."

"No, he'd have been shipped out a long time ago. Still, it got better than that. During the civil war in Sri Lanka in 2009 there was a huge demonstration in the same place that went on for months. They had to close the area to traffic at times as a mini-city sprang up."

"Really?"

"Yeah. It showed the law for what it was, a bit pointless

in the face of peaceful protest. Now I'm not saying you have to shut parts of a city down, but there is definitely a place for it and it can be effective in waking people up to issues that need to be discussed, or at the very least might bother politicians with a democratic conscience."

"That past ability to protest is all very interesting but doesn't answer the question of why people didn't object when elections were cancelled. Why were there no demonstrations then? If enough people had become involved, surely the government would have had to acknowledge they were doing something wrong?"

"There were plenty of people objecting to begin with but there wasn't the same dedication to going against the grain as there had been in previous decades. The government found they could more or less keep the population content by controlling security, information and money. It would have been easier for them if the economy had been better but by 2020 people had begun to adapt to the idea that their living standards were never going to be as good as they were fifteen years before. So all they had to do was manage the application of dissent, as a leaked document from the time put it."

"Sounds creepy. How did they do that?"

"Monitoring of people considered to be anti-government had been going on for a long time but advances in technology meant the police and security service could put less effort in once they knew who they were targeting. The average person didn't know whether they were being watched or not but the popular assumption was that everyone was and people modify their behaviour when they know they're being observed, often to conform to a socially acceptable norm. Combine that with emergency powers to detain anyone deemed a threat and their task became particularly easy. When elections were cancelled, there were protests but the problem the government had was that they couldn't be seen taking white English folk off the streets in the same way they had with Asian, African or Middle Eastern people, so they just became more cunning.

"Public opinion wasn't entirely against The Central Cabinet as the simple logic of there not being any bombings since 2018 made it look like all their efforts were working. Their media cronies helped distribute that message when they saw the opportunity to regain some power and the unspoken pact was that they could continue making money by going back to ravaging the privacy of celebrities, as long as they reported the government's line. Of course not all did, but those newspapers pretty much don't exist anymore, at least not in this country.

"Protesting had also become a fairly splintered activity by then as there were so many single issues that many organisations campaigned for just one thing rather than broader issues. So, when it came to what protests there were, the government set about discrediting the organisers, or they'd grab a few people off the streets and cite them for being part of an illegal march. All public gatherings of more than ten people were banned without permission, so when the police dragged otherwise law-abiding people to the station and quoted various regulations at them, making clear what effect further participation could have on their lives, most started to think again about whether they should have been there. Word spread about the official attitude and when some of the leaders were arrested and thrown in jail, fear swelled. After a few months of keeping to that pattern, complimented by a few nasty newspaper editorials, the idea percolated that the unpatriotic act of protesting wasn't going to be tolerated, leaving those that did open to criticism from within their social circle, and perhaps even at risk of losing their jobs.

"Pretty soon the numbers dwindled and a couple of years later the silencing of the most vocal critics in the media and The Stability Laws allowed the government to do as they pleased. Obviously some people were still wildly unhappy about the removal of democratic processes but they were too afraid to speak up. Those who did were detained and never really heard from again, apart from an occasional smuggled note or vague news that they were alive."

"Sent to the camps?"

"Ah, maybe not as it happens. The uncomfortably racist nature of all this comes to the fore again. The white British people who refused to shut up are rumoured to be in normal prisons, places like Wormwood Scrubs or Holloway, where they're segregated from the everyday criminals in what are called Emergency Blocks. All the authorities want is their silence, and jail is enough to achieve that."

"But if this is really a kind of war, does that mean the

government have won just by getting rid of opposition?"

"Not necessarily. Remember that you're still being told in school about The Activists. The government need to present them as a threat just in case young people are tempted by the idea of protest. Don't assume it's over just because some battles have been won. Regardless of the power of The Central Cabinet and security service, they can't watch every single place or every single person."

"But the only remaining protest comes from The Activists?"

"Yes, but in a very different way as they have to remain hidden. I mean they're obviously anti-government so the description of them in official reports is accurate, but it's far more subtle than that. Hopefully you're starting to see another side to what's happened over the last ten years or so."

"A bit, yes. It's not as clear as it's presented in school."

"Exactly, so think of The Activists in the same way. They've been labelled by the government and selective history has been given to the public about how they're bad for Stability, but it isn't as straightforward as them causing trouble for the sake of it, they're fighting for what they believe in, and in the past they might well have convinced other people just by providing an alternate view. Sometimes they were as guilty as the next bunch of cherry-picking their arguments but that's no different to the socially acceptable history that's taught to you and your friends."

"So we're only getting one side?"

"Correct."

Who owns all the oranges?

"And in order to form a balanced opinion, we'd need the rest of the information, and that's what The Activists could provide?"

"In a manner of speaking, yes, but they can't because as a generic group they've been outlawed, almost silencing them. But answer me this, what does an Activist stand for, who is this standardised person presented as a grave threat to the nation?"

"I'm not sure."

"Exactly, you're just told they're bad. Shouldn't you be allowed to make up your own mind about it?"

"I guess so, but it's impossible to hear their views."

"That's my point. The longer this system becomes established as the norm here, the more difficult it becomes to get another perspective. Occasionally I hear a government or news site has been taken over and information posted about what's happening around the country, but it's rare anything's up for very long. It's great because some people are bound to have seen it and if even a few people question if all this is for the best, then that's a good thing. Bringing down the government and giving people a say can probably only happen three ways. The Central Cabinet could decide to give up power and hold elections, but that will never happen because the longer a totalitarian regime are in power, the more crimes they commit against their people, and the more likely they are to be held savagely to account if ousted. Second, a sizeable majority get sick of living powerlessly within the state and a violent revolution occurs. Also unlikely as most people now live in fear of what might happen if they get stopped speeding. Third and unfortunately most likely is the long game."

"How would that work?"

"Well, the people who can, exiles abroad or those working underground here, slowly chip away at the system, and not necessarily violently. There will always be people who believe an armed struggle is the only way but that strengthens the government because they get to put more military on the streets and fear in the mind. Attacks that show The Stability System up as cruel and incompetent like releasing facts about the camps or satirical rewrites of official statements are just as effective at undermining the self-elevated status of our rulers. Or they could target the companies that run everything by interrupting their processes. Most of them have procedures for dealing with that kind of disruption but they're usually badly tested so often have weaknesses that can be exploited.

"Eventually if there are enough of these that are high profile enough to expose flaws, people will become braver and perhaps even join in. The idea would be for subtle subversion to reach a critical mass so individuals on the inside begin to reconsider their involvement. Then and only then should people take to the streets, when they're sure the government no longer has the power to stop them. Like I said it's a long game, and it's doubtful whether everyone has the patience for it. Even the loose grouping called The Activists is mostly interested in overthrowing the government tomorrow, and that's understandable, but I just don't see how it can work against the kind of unaccountable brutality that exists today."

"So many Activists would prefer if people rose up and fought on the streets?"

"Those are the rumours I hear but at the moment the power lies with the state, which is likely to come out on top in any conflict. It's the wrong time for violence, if there's ever a right time. This government has already shown their willingness to do whatever they think is necessary to keep the population under control and the majority of the people calling for an uprising don't live in the country, so it's easy for them to cry for bloodshed. It's a bit different for people who actually live here to put themselves and their families at risk."

"Dad, we get told in school that the defence of the country should be our primary concern and that includes protecting the principles behind The Stability System. What you're talking about is an assault on the state. Whatever about an uprising, wouldn't attacking the processes that keep the country running cause some sort of anarchy?"

"I suppose it would for a while, but it depends how it's done. Looking at other revolutions over the last forty years or so there has usually been some kind of volatility immediately afterwards. Now, I'm not saying that Britain is going to be different but there are many who remember that the country was stable before any of this happened. I hope that when the current bunch fall, as I'm sure they will one day, those people will have the foresight to say, 'Look, we need to be sensible about this, take it slowly and maintain some sort of order while society is repaired'. Who knows, the so-called Activists may be able to take control while we wait for elections. It can be done because it's been done in other places. It just requires will and the suspension of egos."

"Do you think they'll be able to stay out of the hands of the authorities long enough to do anything?"

"Good question. I imagine anybody based here is as secretive as the organisations that are hunting them. Exiles in Scotland and Ireland live in fear of drone attacks so keep moving around, and those countries have become less accommodating to British refugees since the government started making noises about reintegrating them into the UK. Aside from the historic implications of invading Ireland, Scotland has only been independent for about fifteen years and even though they're sure about not giving up their democracy for The Stability System, they also know that if British forces marched across the border they'd be overrun. The opposition have already been forced to disperse or stay hidden so if they had to move somewhere else, it would probably weaken them further. It's often just small groups or even individuals and as the government have the balance of power it's unlikely they'll bring about change."

"Is it true what the information clips say, that they may walk among us, that they could be our neighbours, friends or family?"

"That's just another fear-inducing ruse, and not a very original one. The best example would be during the 1950s in the US. A similar tactic was used to try and make it seem like communists and homosexuals, that era's supposed enemies, were trying to infiltrate the state. It suits the government to have everybody worrying about threats that may or may not exist, rather than focussing on the fact that their ability to have a say has been removed. I'm sure there are people hidden in plain sight who work underground to try and counter the propaganda, but you shouldn't assume it's everyone or even that they're harmful. The more you fear, the more it allows the message to be dictated, so when you hear of another attack on the nation it's best not to be too scared. It's in the interests of the government to have the majority of the population think we're at war. It gives them the freedom to remove opposition without accountability if they can point to a defined group that's causing trouble and claim they've captured or killed its members, thus making the country safer."

Cassie sat quietly for a moment.

"You realise this goes against everything I've ever been taught," she said.

"I'm aware of that but you did ask."

"That's true. I guess I didn't expect the answer to be so ... corrupting."

"I don't think you're being corrupted, merely educated about what happened to our democracy. You should try not to worry about it too much. It's just good to be aware that not everything in life is as plain as it seems."

One hot, bothersome day in July 2025 I answered the door to a smartly-dressed man in his early twenties, stood smiling cheerfully on the doorstep.

"Hello," I said, "What can I do for you?"

"Good afternoon Mr. O'Dwyer, my name is Quentin and I'm calling on behalf of Stable Interface Solutions. We've been retained by the Ministry for Stability to provide additional monitoring bandwidth over the coming months and our aim is to provide improved workflows along with a more personal presence for external customers during this period of enhanced interaction."

I looked blankly at him.

"What the fuck are you on about?" I said.

"Sir, please," he said, smiling, "let's not get off to a bad start. You've been allocated a higher frequency of sit-downs and I will be carrying them out on behalf of the Ministry."

"But you're not from the other company, the one that comes every month now?"

"Stability Interrogation Services? No, we're a new player in the market acting on opportunities created by recent deregulations in the Stability industry and an increased awareness of the potential for unwanted incidents."

"I take it you're replacing the other lot then."

"No sir, they are still scheduled to carry out sit-downs with you. We're a complimentary service."

"And what is it you're going to do differently?"

"We believe our interrogation techniques will provide additional efficiencies to the Ministry as well as a more positive interaction with subjects. May I come in?"

"What if I say no?"

He paused, momentarily unsure of himself.

"What reason could you have to say no?" he said.

"I don't know who you are. You've just turned up on my doorstep and said you're going to do the same thing another similarly named company does but more frequently. Forgive me but it seems nonsensical that even more money is being wasted on something as pointless as asking me the same questions over and over again."

"Sir, I've been trained in conflict resolution and empathy techniques but I must also warn you that I am carrying a personal protection device that communicates directly with an SES patrol in the area. As we're going to be doing this on a regular basis, I'd prefer if I didn't have to start by calling them. Here is my identification which should be adequate under the circumstances."

"I suppose you better come in then."

He strode irritatingly into the living room and sat on the sofa.

"So how long have you worked for thingy?" I said, sitting down across from him.

"Stable Interface Solutions. I'm enrolled on their graduate trainee program so just the last month. You're my first solo interrogation as it happens."

"Great. What do you have to study at university to get that job?"

"Psychology and art history. This is an exciting entry level position from which I hope to move quickly into more senior roles and eventually build a career as a consultant."

"It's good to have ambition. Best of luck with that."

"Thank you sir. If we could just speed things up a bit, I'll

run through my questions for today. Shouldn't take too long."

"No doubt."

"Super," he said, happily taking a tablet out of his shoulder bag.

"Have you ever been a member of The Activists Mr. O'Dwyer?"

"No."

"Splendid," he said, tapping the tablet. "Have you been approached by anyone claiming to be part of any Activist network?"

"No."

"Tremendous," he said with another tap. "Have you recently written or distributed any material that might be considered anti-Stability?"

"No."

"Wonderful."

He looked me up and down and then around the room. He furiously tapped for twenty or thirty seconds.

"Apologies for the delay Mr. O'Dwyer," he said when he stopped, "but I just needed to take some environmental details to confirm your habitation situation."

"What does that mean?"

"Just a few details about your home for our database and I'll also take a couple of pictures."

"Pictures?"

"Yes, it's company policy that we take a visual record of the subject away from every visit to attach to their file. I'm also required to capture your bookshelf to ensure it contains no unwanted items."

"Right. Do you want me to pose?"

"That won't be necessary sir," he said, smiling.

He stood up, pointed his tablet at me and then the bookshelf.

"Right sir, that's all I need today. I'll be off but will see you sometime next week."

"Do you know when?"

"I'm afraid not. For security reasons I can't give the exact day or time."

"What if I'm not in?"

"I'll leave a calling card and come again but please be aware that failure to be present during the second attempt at service delivery may result in a capture notice being issued to the SES."

"So I pretty much can't leave my home anymore."

"No sir, you're a Cat-3 so have extensive freedoms. However the financial projections in our contract are based on only a small number of lapsed interrogations so we are authorised to use enforcement to carry out our duties efficiently."

"Splendid. See you the next time then."

"Goodbye Mr. O'Dwyer," he said as he walked towards the door.

"Goodbye," I said, not seeing him out.

I sat on the sofa he'd just vacated and stared into space. It occurred to me to check he hadn't stolen anything as I wasn't sure whether he was a con-artist or not. Frighteningly it seemed he might not be and that was what youthful ambition looked like now.

"You know," I said, getting up to put the kettle on, "the real problem is that people have basic needs like water, food and shelter. Once you provide a certain level of sustenance then perhaps the ability to protest or vote becomes less important."

"But not everyone can afford those things."

"No, and as I've said before, there used to be help for people who found themselves in a bad situation. The majority of assistance given to the most deprived in society now comes from charities, food banks and volunteers though on a very informal basis because the government disapprove of its embarrassing connotations. The dismantling of much of the social welfare system by the Tory/UKIP coalition was the ultimate triumph of ideology, ignoring evidence and media sensationalism. Decisions fell into the hands of private companies who, in order to make a profit, set targets for how much money could be distributed, effectively putting a limit on how many people would be helped. It's the ultimate cause of what are now called The Projects, an insincere term imported from the US that makes it sound like someone's trying to do something about it. In reality, they're ghettos where there's very little law and order, high unemployment, bad education and intense poverty. The government ignore it because they don't have to do anything apart from contain anything that might look like opposition."

"I've heard you and Mum talk about those areas before, haven't there always been places like that?"

"Yes, but the destitution is more concentrated now."

"I don't think I know anyone who lives anywhere like that."

"That's probably true but it doesn't mean you should ignore their existence. People your age living in the ghettos are just as deserving of food, shelter and a decent education as you are."

"Are schools that bad there? Why aren't they given the same opportunities to learn as I am?"

"Because education is mostly run by private industry now and they see more hassle than money in the ghettos. Our taxes still pay for most of it, but for the last thirty years or so there's been a gradual shift to giving control to companies or individuals. As with everything else, once something becomes a little bit acceptable, it can be expanded to become the norm and the Tory/LibDem coalition did that. They allowed anyone to get government funding as long as they kept to a basic curriculum and certain standards, so schools could be set up for personal or political reasons and earn money from their interaction with the state. In the early days some were shut down or taken over by the regulator but over time, as the system became more and more private, the rules became looser. Today all they have to do is teach Maths, English and Stability Education, which is galling."

"Why?"

"Citizenship classes in the days of democracy were quite limited. If people my age had been taught how our systems worked so they understood better what rights they had, then maybe politicians might not have gotten away with removing them so easily. Instead most people were blindly apathetic to what happened over the twenty odd years leading up to The Emergency and I think that had a lot to do with ignorance of the effects of the laws that were being passed. If they'd known what they were losing maybe they wouldn't have been so docile.

"Anyway, it's too late. Education is now something that's done for profit and ideology rather than children and society. It's based on much narrower parameters than it used to be. Sure, you learn the basics, but nothing that allows you to think for yourself. Foreign languages, artistic subjects and so-called incompatible literature have been banished as unnecessary, meaning your generation don't develop any curiosity or the ability to question the facts presented to you. It'll only get worse if you go to university. Rote learning is the norm now and intellectual dissent hasn't been tolerated for years."

"Why are we having this conversation then, if people my age aren't capable of querying what they're taught?"

"Because you've grown up in a house that's always appreciated a good question."

"I see, why thank you. So children in the ghettos are just ignored?"

"Yeah, and it's a short-sighted view that will probably cause problems in the future, should we ever emerge from this mess. The state run schools are now such a minor part of the system that there's just a tiny number of staff in the Department for Education that deals with them. They also receive a lot less money than privatised schools because the funding rules favour schools where, and this is a real quote from the 2022 Education Laws, 'a benefit to the future economy and social fabric of the state can be demonstrated'. Not only is that a fairly vague statement to begin with but it's also used to justify lack of investment in troublesome areas by saying that because they don't provide much tax revenue, they should receive less investment. It's an almost perfect example of dehumanising people in favour of short term profit that creates a vicious circle of bad education and insufficient opportunities."

"How can people accept living like that?"

"They don't. The ghettos are the places where riots happen most, but generally the daily struggle to survive means they don't have the time or energy to do anything but continue to exist. They work the longest hours for the least money, if they work at all, and pay exploitative rents to landlords who don't maintain their properties, leaving bugger all for food and heating. Back in the early part of the century there was a movement that tried to force companies to pay people better, which eventually even some politicians supported. It made a lot of sense, wages high enough to live on mean the government don't have to pay out benefits from the social welfare budget, saving money for other things. A lot of companies did sign up and even the council in London insisted on its contractors paying people a living wage for a while, but once our rulers didn't have to answer to the public attempts to make life better were dropped."

"But it's not just people in the ghettos that struggle with money."

"Of course not, everybody has to budget, that's just a fact of life, especially now. But if you have a job or are lucky enough to be considered for help and you still can't afford to eat then something's wrong. However, politically and economically the state needs an underclass to do the most menial jobs and they also serve as another handy group to victimise when a scapegoat is needed. There are more people in what are called the middle classes that need to be appeased and they provide revenue to the government so they present the ghettos as a danger that can't be fixed and needs controlling, rather than people who could have better lives if they had access to the same opportunities as the rest of us, or even just a small helping hand."

"There are lots of rumours in school about the ghettos being full of Activists."

"That may or may not be true. As you say, it's a rumour."

"Ok. Again though, what about all the people who don't live there? I understand that sometimes money is tight but everyone around here has a phone, a television, a decent enough home. Why don't they see the injustice of what's happening?"

"Some probably do, in fact some definitely do, but this is no different to speaking out against the camps or disappearances. The government don't want a discussion about it and presenting the ghettos as hell around the corner keeps the majority from thinking of the people who live there as fellow human beings who need the same things that they so comfortably have, like food and a reasonable place to live."

"Not a phone and television?"

"They won't keep you alive, though the government have noticed that a significant slice of the population can be kept content as long as they have the ability to buy things. It's still an important factor in many people's lives and one it sometimes seems they've given up their right to vote for. Of course there was a time when that type of hasty consumerism was worse because people had more money, but it's true that many still like to have the latest gadgets and the ability to share their status with others, though that isn't as popular as it once was."

"It still amazes me that everyone used to live their lives in public. Every thought, every whim, every photo. There's nobody my age would consider doing that anymore."

"Yes, but that's because you're all vaguely aware of the consequences of surveillance and dissent, plus you can't have a phone at your age anyway."

"True, and I think I'm going to regret saying this, but isn't that to protect us from ourselves?"

"Amazing what years of indoctrination can do to you, but no, it's mostly to try and stop protest among young people who by the age of twenty-one will have finished school, college or university, probably the most open community-based experiences they'll have in their lives. Not allowing people to have phones until after that reduces their ability to organise themselves quickly. Now, you may not believe this but young people used to protest locally and nationally about whatever the issues of the day were. Often gatherings were channelled through the student union or social media sites so the first step was pulling funding for unions, removing places where students could congregate or make collective decisions. At the same time, the police increased their presence on campuses as well, something that hadn't really happened before but meant that even before 2018, they were carrying out security and immigration checks in universities and creating an early impression of a police state by spying on and infiltrating student groups.

"The next step, as part of the Communication Protection Laws, was the banning of mobile phones. As almost all other online activity happened through university networks, it was easy to monitor and block. A few high profile expulsions were all that was needed after that to ensure compliance. Now there's a surveillance unit on every campus, conformity has been more or less ingrained. Making repression normal when people are young means they're less likely to buck against the system when they're older. The government have had to spend more time bothering people like me because I have more of the old ways in my mind than any of your friends, who've grown up being told this is the way things are. The danger is that your generation will never be able to understand that a country can be run in the interests of its citizens."

"So when people get a job they don't question what

happens around them, as long as they have a certain level of comfort in their lives?"

"Pretty much."

"I find that hard to believe, lots of people my age are really unhappy about what they see around them."

"Maybe, but what will they actually do about it and how likely are they to go against the power of the state after they've left the relative comfort of home and have to fend for themselves."

"I don't know, maybe you're right. What about the people who don't go to university?"

"There's no real difference between how people are treated in university, colleges or apprenticeships when it comes to surveillance and compliance. If you want a job you have to publicly conform or end up in the lowest paid positions being treated less than humanely."

"But surely when people have more independence, when they start to earn money and make decisions about their lives, they'll realise they should be able to have more alternatives," she said.

"In theory yes, but freedom of choice is a very subjective thing. I would prefer to have the option of voting to get rid of a government I don't like, write analyses of the advantages and disadvantages of their policies or take them to court for wrongful imprisonment. Others are happy with a new mobile phone and the colour of paint on their living room wall. It's not in people's nature to confront the system – they prefer to moan about it from their armchairs instead. Of course there are exceptions but most just conform, which is a type of choice I suppose. If you want to be able to have that comfortable life we've talked about, however reduced it is these days, you need to put up with doing things you don't like. It can often depend on who you work for of course, but most employers are the same nowadays. It's been that way for a long time and The Stability System helps with that."

Who owns all the oranges?

The years after the 2025 uprising were quiet. Most people just got on with their lives, trying to make ends meet as the near twenty year long depression kept wages down and prices up. Restrictions on the arts meant there wasn't much to take people's minds off the bleakness around them. High streets had never recovered fully from the crash and the deep-rooted economic order meant only the large chains survived, adding to the homogenised gloom.

Cassie reached her teens but had withdrawn from the world after Iqbal's disappearance. She did have friends but seemed to prefer not to stray too far from her Mum's or mine, burying herself in what books were allowed. It was hard to know if this was worrying or just the way teenagers were when their choices were limited – there were no psychologists or sociologists willing to comment on the effects of totalitarianism on the adolescent psyche. In spite of our awareness of everything that went on around us, the propaganda-filled media only added to our concerns by showing happy, outgoing young people doing wholesome activities in support of the nation.

Witnessing Iqbal being bundled into a van obviously changed her and it was close to impossible for us to explain it. There was no logic that could justify a twelve-year-old boy being sent to a detention camp for no apparent reason. We chose, rightly or wrongly, not to discuss it in too much detail to try and protect her from the callous reality.

I had a visit from Stability Interrogation Services every month or so and Quentin from Stable Interface Solutions every week, the only joy ever to come out of this being their bewilderment when they happened to turn up at the same time once and couldn't work out who's schedule should have priority. After a long comparison of the rulebooks each of them carried on their tablets, several phone calls with several managers and an escalation to someone in something called the Stability Liaison Office, neither of them interviewed me that day as the time taken to sort out their muddle meant the days rota had been ruined.

When they did manage to fit me into their to-do lists, they'd ask the usual meaningless questions and tap the answers in their tablets. Two or three times a year I'd be taken from the house to the place with the gravel and lavender to answer the same questions when they discovered the now very occasional distributions of what was termed non-governmental information.

The restrictions in the electronic world had created a need for paper newsletters of the kind that existed long before the internet came along. The enterprising would find old printers and get them working again, creating mini-newspapers that could usually only be distributed to a small group, often printed on waste office paper retrieved from recycling bins. Occasionally they'd pass through my hands or I'd see small groups pretending to talk but actually listening to someone reciting the stories from one of them.

It still wasn't enough though as the same people would wait for these intermittent newssheets while everyone else kept their heads down. We were mostly cowed but listening, powerlessly waiting for something to change.

I put two mugs of tea on the kitchen table as Cassie said, "How does The Stability System help keep people in line at work as well? Isn't that separate from the day-to-day pressure from Cabinet?"

"Sort of but they're interlinked in many ways. There's always been a close relationship between government and business, which is necessary in many ways as their expertise is valuable and without them there wouldn't be an economy, but politicians have gradually excluded other voices that might have provided a counterbalance to the ethos of profit above all else."

"What other voices?"

"Charities, trade unions and non-governmental organisations which, like companies, would often have their own agendas but in many cases could provide the other side of an argument and a collective voice, allowing ministers, and the public, to make a balanced decision. Gradually though, their access to ministers was phased out to the point where they were lucky to meet with policymakers at all, whereas organisations that promoted the interests of industry have always been able to get more face time, particularly after the Tory/LibDem coalition passed laws curtailing activities in the run up to elections. Some organisations were limited in the amount they could spend campaigning for an issue and that same bill forced unions to track member details more closely and hand that information over on request, which eventually allowed the government to outlaw them for minor data infringements and the police to target lists of people considered troublemakers.

"Apart from being registered, the commercial lobbyists were allowed to continue steering government in their direction. Remember back to the Blair years when unelected advisers became more powerful than elected MPs; lobbyists gained a similarly disproportionate influence. It could be argued that the ideology of certain politicians had a part to play and individuals certainly did push agendas they believed in but sometimes it wasn't difficult to spot the soft hand on the small of their backs gently pushing them down a certain path. This had happened for decades but became more blatant at the turn of the century. The lobbyists seemed to be in control of making laws for business just as much as the security services were for surveillance, further removing people from the decisions that were made about them. Add to that the fact that many of the groups behind these politician whisperers were donating huge amounts to political parties in the hope of gaining even more influence after an election, and that particular corruption of democracy was complete."

"Unfortunately many of those lobbying companies supplied our water, food, energy and healthcare as well as the less essential things, so there was a need to align the state with private enterprise. However, there have been too many scandals over the years where policies have benefitted companies and not people, which shouldn't happen when it involves things necessary for our survival. The cost of these often goes way past what most people can afford, sometimes because of the way prices fluctuate on global markets but often just because deregulation means they can more or less charge what they want. The ideas behind Stability Economics go back to the 1980s and follow the theory that if industry is allowed to roam freely across the economic plains, making up their own rules as they go to increase profits, then money and better living standards will filter down to workers. Fifty years later, the inequality that fantasy created is still with us."

"I don't understand. If companies are busy they hire people and there are more jobs and therefore money. Right?"

"Of course but it comes back to the point about not paying people enough to live on or even giving them a contract anymore. The spread of wealth within private companies doesn't really trickle down to everyone, it's retained by a few while insecurity floods across the bottom, infecting not just those in the ghettos but a huge swathe of nominally middle class people who can just about endure paying their rent, food and energy bills every month. Many don't know if they'll still have a job from one day to the next now there are no labour laws but that fear and uncertainty is also what keeps them working hard, which companies like. That there's money in the economy according to figures like GDP and per capita income does not mean that everybody is benefitting."

"Ok. I think I see but surely there will always be people who are richer than everyone else."

"Yes and there isn't anything wrong with that as long as they've done something to deserve it and retain some sense of wider responsibility to society. Don't misunderstand me sweetie, without industry people would be even worse off than they are now but power and wealth go hand in hand and those that earn most have dissociated themselves from the rest of us in order to preserve and grow what they alone have, which doesn't automatically provide any benefit to the majority of the population."

"So the theory you're talking about that Stability Economics is based on doesn't necessarily mean country-wide security and prosperity?"

"No and that dogma also gave us the idea that once private enterprise is involved in the running of state bodies everything becomes more efficient, therefore freeing up money to improve citizens' lives. That was just ideological obfuscation though as a big company works no better than a big government department, the difference being that it's easier to see failures in a public entity. In the past, because the civil service worked for everyone, whistleblowers would eventually appear because if something was seriously wrong then somebody's conscience or political slant would trigger a release of information. Companies only have to answer to shareholders but if profits keep rolling in and there are no great scandals, they tend to keep quiet. In more open times, controversies surrounding the way government contracts were carried out were in the news all the time but disgraced companies still bid for and got more jobs even when it wasn't clear what the advantages were."

"We're taught in school that responsibilities needed

to be taken away from the old civil service as it couldn't deal with larger projects economically."

"What else would they teach you? The country used to be split down the middle about what the right way should be but there was always a fairly sizable section of the population who thought privatisation of the things we really needed like health, education, power, water and transport was a bad idea. However, there were also plenty of people who believed that everything should be sold off to reduce the size of the state and their arguments were the ones that took hold. It's made it almost impossible for the country to regain control because the money earned from selling those assets was spent the moment it reached the government's bank account, so there's no possibility of buying anything back. The end result is that if you look a bit deeper at the few services provided to us, where and how we buy things and the links companies have to the people now in control, it's not difficult to see how right some people were to be suspicious of large businesses."

"Why?"

"A few reasons but to begin with, around the turn of the century our ability to buy changed. Technology advanced quickly and new gadgets came out all the time – not just phones, TVs and computers but a whole range of things that people didn't know they needed. The economy was booming, wages were rising and many people suddenly had spare money. The companies that got things right got rich and used to it, so were reluctant to give it up when times got tough. Their lobbyists would make the case for helpful laws and, particularly after the crash, try to convince the ruling parties that the only way to sustain the economy was to give them what they wanted, which was less regulation for the most part. Every government since the 1980s had been unquestioningly pro-business so it wasn't difficult to push through favourable legislation."

Cassie took a sip from her mug and sat back in her chair.

"I'm not sure I understand where this fits in with The Stability System or keeping people under control at work."

"Patience sweetie, I'm getting there. Fast forward a few years to the beginning of the twenties. We're mid-Emergency, elections have been cancelled and the first putrid buds of The Stability System are starting to show. The government need private industry on side in order to keep control, because if the economy collapses that'll be more difficult. There's only so far surveillance and restrictions get you so the best thing a government that lives in a bubble can do is align themselves with the companies that already have access to most of our daily lives in one way or another. Again, many talked about leaving Britain, and some did, but the majority stayed and continued to sell their wares and provide their services as they became ever closer to the politicians that made life easier for them."

"So they supported the removal of our rights?"

"Essentially yes, but this was a time when countries with no discernible levels of democracy were becoming more economically powerful and were still allowed to sell to anyone, supposedly because exposure to countries that bathed in their democracy meant they would eventually open up and give more freedoms to their people. Influence, regrettably, remains with the money, and that made liberty unimportant when it came to economic advancement, so many companies just followed that ethos. People still try to excuse our current lack of rights by referring to Asia and Africa where countries have been prosperous in spite of totalitarianism, but you could just as easily find a country in Europe or South America that hasn't had to go down the road we have to be this moderately successful.

"As for how industry compliments that style of governance you have to look at the huge corporations created over the years by the buying and selling of smaller companies. The cheapest way to run those conglomerates was to have centralised control. For that to work the same style of management and reporting had to be imposed throughout. The guys at the top needed to be able to see at a glance how each part was doing and making the structure rigid made that easier.

"Many people found themselves working for small companies within larger ones but gradually those got lost in the noise. Employees, who once said good morning to the head of their company as they passed in the corridor, were moved to sprawling anonymous offices where they became detached from their work as it often arrived and left electronically without interaction with another human being, allowing companies to reduce costs and increase profits at the expense of a decent working environment.

"As a result workers eventually became a fairly homogenised group of people who were willing to put up with quite a lot of crap. They might go to the pub and have a moan but for the most part they got on with their work as their rights were slowly stripped away, right up to the point in 2022 when all labour laws were formally scrapped. Contrast that with thirty or forty years previously when they'd have been out on strike and you get a sense of how life changed for the average employee. It's travelled from one extreme to the other, though I've been told somewhere in the 1990s employers were better at a bit of give and take. Often if people worked hard and did their jobs to the best of their abilities they were allowed a certain amount of freedom. If they stayed late into the night for weeks, giving up their lives to finish an order or a project, managers were more flexible about staff clawing back some free time when things were more relaxed, allowing a better balance between work and life. It meant people were happier in their jobs because they didn't resent working hard when things were busy, as they knew their boss might turn a blind eye to the odd late morning when things were calmer."

"Sounds sensible. What happened?"

"I suppose to a certain extent the accountants took control and when they looked at the numbers they saw gaps in what people's perceived productivity was. When companies measured their employees per day, regardless of whether that day lasted eight hours or fifteen, they didn't see anything but a day that could be charged to a client. However, when a half day in calmer times was charged to administration because the employee's boss said they could catch up on a bit of sleep after several weeks of hard work, all the accountant saw was wages paid out that couldn't be billed to anyone, which looked like wasted money in the books. As companies began to rely on software systems to track efficiency, the middle ground between employer and employee disappeared as the need for justification of every hour, or even minute, became important to show those at the top that everything was running economically. It was part of the dehumanisation in the workplace that destroyed some of the personal relationship people had with their bosses, as well as being the beginning of companies viewing their workers as property rather than a real live human resource that they could trust and rely on."

"Great, something for me to look forward to. So being able to put up with a reasonable amount of crap to gain a certain level of comfort is why everybody sat back and let democracy die?"

"That's only the beginning of the crap they now tolerate and the level of comfort isn't as high as you might think. Link it back to the other things we've talked about today – lower pay, the control of protest among students and the limited education they receive. When people leave university or college they generally start on lower wages but there's also a belief they'll go up over time. All that still works the same with the difference these days being the level of debt graduates have, meaning they begin their working life in an already bad financial position so need years to regain a bit of balance, but twenty years of a rubbish economy means pay hasn't gone up enough to cover the increased cost of living, let alone pay back loans, so most people are locked into a life of merely covering their expenses from month to month.

"Britain has also had some of the longest working hours in Europe for decades, meaning stress and mental tiredness are a fact of life. Couple that with no legal requirement to offer holidays anymore. Most companies have cut them back significantly giving very few people the ability to escape abroad, not just because you need a Foreign Office permit but because they can't afford the time or money, handily not exposing them to what might seem like a better life elsewhere.

"All these things breed a tired, dejected and insecure workforce but people have to earn to eat so they keep plodding on, and they've already come out of college or university fairly compliant so life is easy for a company that wants the most from their employees for the least amount of money. Now that centralised control I talked about is ideal for this because it fails to see the human side of workers. They become nothing more than numbers on a spreadsheet with a value of expected productivity attached to them, and that allows those at the top to distance themselves emotionally from the reality of conditions at the bottom.

"That's made worse by the layers of control most large

companies employ. They see no problem in numerous managers fulfilling minor roles because each will produce a report on the area they have responsibility for, which justifies having them there. The problem is that it requires a lot of them to write all the reports the head of a company wants but the expense means there often isn't money to do the actual work, so the people at the bottom are overwhelmed. In order to validate the structure, there might be one or two people at the bottom of a department but five or six managers with varying responsibilities vying for their time. As each of them stresses about protecting their middling positions under pressure from the top, the strain on workers is greater as they have to spend more time dealing with politics and unnecessary meetings than doing their jobs.

"Take that point, where people are harassed and unhappy at work, where they get by at home by affording to eat and buy the occasional treat, and then lay The Stability System on top. A person who's already lost interest in what the government can do for them and chooses to find joy in life wherever they can isn't going to care about the removal of democracy, something they thought was just about voting every few years and appeared to make minimal difference to their lives anyway. The other important elements of a balanced state had already been badly damaged – the courts, the parliamentary committees, the press and the ability to protest – laying down the blueprint for the excessive control people now experience from both government and their employers."

In 2029 a determined fight-back began but with fewer violent clashes or bombings than there had been in 2025. Electronic attacks on infrastructure and attempts to influence or change the information most people were seeing were common. The government were emphasising the fight for the stability of the nation when they had to but there were signs they were starting to weaken until they retaliated fiercely.

It was becoming increasingly difficult to hide my contempt for the corporations that called at my door. Perhaps this was why I was taken to the room in the country more often, probably every couple of months now, sometimes for days. The questions remained the same as the attacks increased – I was still accused of writing anti-government articles by a piece of software and further studies showed the likelihood of me having changed my views to support the regime as being negligible, so perhaps there was some accuracy in their idiocy.

The interrogation techniques became harsher, from daytime meetings with my wiry old friend and others to keeping me awake for several nights while a succession of different people passed through the room, which became increasingly raw as sleep deprivation kicked in.

My spirit was breaking though I tried to hide that from Cassie. It was difficult as the increasing pressure began to chip away at me and the physical signs of intimidation began to show. I got less work, probably because I'd been blacklisted, but I had some money from the few moderately successful books I'd written so still had the means to live, but boredom was getting to me.

In November 2029 I was reclassified as a Category-2 enemy 'as a precautionary measure'. I was electronically tagged and confined to a small circle around the house, plus a daily trip to the high street between the hours of two and four, but I needed special permission to go further afield which was never given. I was reminded that I should consider myself controlled from now on.

I got up to put the mugs in the sink as Cassie thought.

"This is kind of depressing," she said.

"Yes, it is," I replied, leaning against the working top, "but I still haven't gotten to the crucial point yet, the means by which the larger companies maintain their positions of power, not just over us but the government as well. Lobbying and political donations are only the beginning of that story."

"It gets worse?"

"Oh yes. Around the mid tens, the ultimate private industry sideswipe on democracy came in the form of international trade agreements. Years were spent negotiating deals to make trade between countries easier, which is no bad thing for any economy and did result in the increased exports that the government now rely on to keep us afloat. However, they also handed the judging of disputes to industry rather than courts, weakening the judicial system long before The Central Cabinet sidelined them. The new way of working meant if a company disagreed with a democratically passed law because it might impact on their profits, regardless of the benefits to the population as a whole, they could take a country to a panel that existed outside normal legal processes and ask for damages. The agreements were designed to compensate businesses from countries with which the trade deals had been signed but, because of the globalised nature of trade, large corporations had offices everywhere so they could just choose a territory that had one of these deals with their target nation and launch their suit from there. When Britain was still part of the European Union, the bloc as a whole signed several of these agreements with the US, China and others but unfortunately when we left, the Tory/UKIP coalition chose to stay part of that system until they'd renegotiated the terms. In the end nothing changed, they just altered the names on the documents, swapping one set of regulations they had no power over for another, putting the business community in control instead of the EU."

"So when those international giants of industry chose to stay in Britain, it wasn't because they had faith in the return of democracy and the rule of law. No, they saw an opportunity for enormous short term profits. With each new Cabinet decree, from banning certain books and films to controlling the media or forbidding mobiles for young people, a new claim would be submitted requesting compensation for future profits lost. By 2025, there were so many restrictions that the government owed hundreds of billions of pounds in compensation and had no option but to look at how they were going to settle."

"I don't understand. They do what they want. Couldn't they just refuse?"

"Without the very companies that were suing them the jobless rate would have been even higher, tax revenues from workers would have fallen and they might have had trouble paying the police and military, two elements any totalitarian regime needs. The cost of goods would have soared and shops would have suffered shortages without the ability to purchase food from abroad. Revolution would be that much closer if the majority of the population began to struggle. The companies knew this and called the government's bluff by threatening to pull out of Britain."

"And that worked?"

"Yes, unfortunately."

"So how much did they get?"

"Almost nothing."

"What?"

"The government paid close to nothing in monetary terms, mostly because they didn't have it and couldn't borrow as easily as they once had. Instead they signed away any remaining assets the state owned and then the government departments themselves. The deal was that the taxes each working person paid would go the same direction they always had but almost the entire country would be run by the companies which were owed money. Hence the Department for Education is leased to a firm which charges the government to use its offices for the small number of state schools nobody wants control of. The health service had been sold off by the time of The Emergency anyway but other things like the BBC, environmental services, roads, prisons, and of course the camps, are all run by private companies, who in turn often run the departments that control them. The civil service no longer exists as a service to civilians, but as a collection of profit generators that provide a partial service to the people who are supposedly their customers, us. The idea of a social contract between people and government is gone, cast aside by the loss of state bodies that generations of taxpayers put money, effort and ideas into building.

"One of the worst examples is what happened to our parks, commons and woodlands. You probably remember when we used to drive to the countryside at the weekend. All those places we visited when you were a child used to be free for everyone, then sometime in the mid tens a cost was put on nature, supposedly to stop it from being destroyed as the theory was that if it had a monetary value then that would fit better with the way everyone viewed the world and they'd have more respect for it. It was a warped logic really when you consider access to nature had long been found to improve the mental wellbeing of a society so wasn't necessarily worth anything in pounds. The obsession in those days though was to value everything but once they did, when the time came to pay off the corporate debts, all of it went. There was a charter that said they must be available for public use, but there was nothing that said it had to be free or couldn't be sold on, hence the reason there are a lot of oil derricks in our national parks now. I used to feel minor rage every time I paid for my yearly permit for the Downs when I was still allowed to go there but I did because it was important to me to be able to still have access to it. I was lucky to be able to afford it I suppose, but it was a small freedom I treasured.

"You've grown up with this so are used to seeing a company logo come with everything you do. Departments and services that were once run by the state are now in private hands and the government call those who run the country their partners. They certainly are, but ones who make a profit by ignoring the fact that they're not just taking our money from a brutal regime, but aiding it in its everyday quest to control us.

"That was the price we paid when a small cabal of politicians decided to take over. They don't have absolute control, given it's shared with their corporate collaborators, but I've always assumed there's plenty of cash changing hands in the background, so the economic authoritarianism is entrenched. The money we help make goes round and round. We work, get paid, buy things and pay the government taxes. They then pay companies to run the country and a portion of it gets taken as profit and moved offshore never to be seen again. The fact that there's no societal growth because the money made is never reinvested in anything beneficial results in a kind of flat economy subjugation, not just of us as citizens as our services deteriorate, but of The Central Cabinet as well though they don't really realise it because in the short term, times are good for them."

I sat back down across from Cassie.

"What about the smaller companies that don't have these big centralised operations?" she said, "Where do they fit into this?"

"They deal with the bigger ones, who dictate the terms, and remember the police and Ministry for Stability are private as well so can be used to enforce whatever is most favourable to the more influential companies. The government, reduced as it is, retains the top jobs across the board and control of the Treasury and the Bank of England, plus the military and Singular Security Service, but everything else is gone. We are an experiment in what happens when private enterprise runs an entire country. It has free reign to make decisions in the departments it controls with minimal oversight from ministers. There are no restrictions on power in either government or industry anymore as there are no democratic processes. No courts, no press, no votes. In fact, it's probably wrong to call it an experiment. It's more like corporate anarchy."

"Isn't there a danger that the companies might try to take over completely?"

"That hasn't become an issue yet but yes, given their size and financial clout, it is possible a company could move itself into a position to seize control. However, by retaining the two most powerful forces and the money, The Central Cabinet still have the advantage and the conglomerates' inherent weakness of constant middle management power struggles distracts them from looking externally for now. The deal as it stands is that everybody wins except us, the politicians get rich and supposedly rule and businesses get most of the taxes we pay by providing shit services. Realistically, it's unlikely there would be any difference in our lives if they did take over. It would be the same police force, the same secret service, and definitely the same disregard for us as citizens."

"Surely that's the fault of the companies that initially caused this dehumanisation."

"To a certain extent, yes, but don't forget what started all this was a power grab by a bunch of politicians. In the end, it's difficult to see what might have happened if we'd remained democratic, maybe industry would have taken over the running of the country anyway. They were half way there by the time emergency powers came in so it's difficult to predict what the outcome might have been if elections hadn't been cancelled. Perhaps if we ever get out of this it can somehow be reversed, people will say never again, and your generation will see the error of it all. But for now, it is what it is, and we all have to put up with it."

Jane called around early one evening.

"Hi, can I come in?" she said.

"Of course, come on through, can I get you a drink of anything?"

"No, I'm fine ... ok, maybe a glass of wine if you've got one."

"Sure, I'll join you. So what can I do for you, don't often see you round these parts?" I said as she followed me through to the kitchen.

"Cassie's at the cinema and I think we need to talk about her. I'm worried. She doesn't seem to have much interest in anything these days."

"You mean she's a teenager."

"No, it's not just that. I can't get any sense out of her or even find out what's going on in her life. I wondered if you had any idea what might be wrong."

"You're looking at me a bit accusingly."

"I know she loves her visits, but I've noticed in the last couple of months she's become even more withdrawn, more thoughtful, particularly after being here. I just thought you might know what's going on with her?"

"I don't know. She's still the same inquisitive intelligent Cassie she's always been."

I paused as I poured the wine.

"There's something you're not telling me. Don't think I can't see it," she said.

"What?"

"What's going on? Tell me."

"Nothing is going on."

"What do you two talk about when she's here?"

"The usual stuff, what she might do after school, what's going on in her life."

"Well, it's nice she shares that stuff with you."

"Jane, don't be like that."

"Maybe you can share a bit of it with me, given she's my child too."

"Look, she's just a bit confused about life that's all. This isn't an easy place for a teenager to grow up, bombarded by propaganda and surrounded by cruelty."

"Maybe but you know as well as anyone we have to steer her down a careful path."

"Yes, but it's also not fair to restrict her view."

A sudden realisation crept across her face.

"You've been explaining the past to her, haven't you?" she said.

"Jane ..."

"For fuck's sake, we agreed to tell her sometime but now is not that time. You can't just do this without consulting me."

She glared at me before storming to the living room.

"She's growing up and understands a lot about what's going on around her," I said as I moved through and sat down. "She has a lot of questions and yes, I've answered some of them. Isn't it better that she hears it here rather than trying to find answers out on the street?"

"You're putting her in danger, she shouldn't know these things."

"She hasn't told anyone what we've been talking about."

"How do you know?"

"Ok, I don't, but I'm pretty sure she hasn't. She understands the dangers."

"She's seventeen! She doesn't understand anything about it."

"I think you should give her more credit, she's had one of her friends and his whole family disappear and her father keeps vanishing for days. I think she's well aware of what's going on. You can't possibly think I started the conversation."

"I suppose not, but I still think you should have consulted me before telling her all this. I have a right to know."

"Ok, I accept that to a certain extent. I guess I thought it might be safer if only she and I knew."

"Maybe, but you have to see how this concerns me."

"You think it doesn't worry me."

"So why tell her now, why not wait until she's older?"

"I don't know, I suppose I wanted her to know why I think everything that's happening is wrong."

"It's lovely that you want to bond with your daughter and massage your ego by passing on your ideas but you could have waited a few years."

"Maybe I don't have a few years."

We sipped our wine for a moment.

"I'm sorry," she said, *"I understand, but you still should have involved me before you began to fill her head with the kind of stories that might get her in trouble. If you disappear, I'm the one who'll be left behind to pick up the pieces of Cassie's life."*

"I know."

We sat quietly until Jane broke the silence.

"How bad are the interrogations getting?" she said.

"The truth is, the questions are generally the same but I'm being held for longer each time and the tactics they're using

to try and break me are getting worse. I pretty much didn't sleep for four nights last week. I find myself getting weaker and weaker as time goes on."

"What are they trying to get out of you?"

"Nothing in particular as far as I can tell, it's just a way of breaking your spirit so you don't have the will to object."

"I thought they might have left you alone by now."

"I probably don't do myself any favours. I'm a little too honest and I don't go along with that babble they speak or the constant need to adhere to procedure. There's a lot going on at the moment and I think they're nervous, which doesn't help."

"Maybe it's time to be more careful."

"I think I'm long past that stage. The irrational nature of it still troubles me. I find it hard to ignore and particularly difficult not to throw back in their faces."

"I heard Liz, Paul and Frank have disappeared."

"Yeah."

"Do you know where they are?"

"No, it's too difficult to get that kind of information these days. The only thing I did hear is that people who know each other are being separated. I guess it stops them discussing anything that might be unacceptable, but unless they build a jail for every person they want out of the way, that's not really going to work."

"In some ways they already have."

"True."

"Do you know if they were really involved in anything?"

"As much as I am."

"It'll crush her if you disappear, you know that don't you?"

"I know, but it's not as if I'll have any choice in the matter.

Guilt is presumed these days, even if it's based on proof from eight years ago judged today."

"Did any of you ever regret doing it, banding together to criticise the government like that, continuing to write as democracy burned so to speak?"

"Not personally, no. Perhaps we were complacent and a tad egotistical in thinking we could do it without the safety net of a major backer but by then most of those were controlled anyway. I regret the effect it's had on my life since, not being able to live with Cassie, and you. It all seems unfair but there are many in a worse position. Look at how long the camps have kept people. I still believe it was the right thing to do, trying to convince them to think again about what they were doing."

"It was, I can't disagree with that, and it's easy with hindsight to say that maybe you shouldn't have taken the risks. Who could have known this is where we'd end up?"

"Indeed. So how much pressure are you under these days?"

"Enough. We don't get figures from the Treasury or the Bank of England anymore. We get a press release that's already analysed the economy for us. Stray away from that official line and you run the risk of disapproval. It doesn't really matter anyway as we couldn't get the information for ourselves even if we tried. All the departments are closed so tightly now that you can't get a whistleblower like you could in the old days. People are too scared of losing their jobs and being marked out as having gone against the system. The fear of being cast into the ghettos is too much."

"Someday somebody will stand up again."

"I'm not so sure anymore."

"Human beings have limits. It can't go on forever like this."

"No, but the history of similar regimes tells us that it might have at least a few decades left to run, probably more than our lifetimes."

"Probably."

"Do you think we did the right thing? With Cassie I mean."

"I'm not sure we could have done anything else. I mean, what were our options? It would have been worse for her seeing all of this happen uncontrollably before her eyes. At least this way, even though she's still had to face things someone her age never should, she's protected from the worst of it. It's a question of the level of dread she has to deal with and this is slightly less."

"You're right but it still troubles me sometimes."

"I think that's only natural but we had to make a decision based on what we thought was best at the time."

"I know. I hope you never resented me for it."

"No, of course not. I agreed, remember. It wasn't like you just pushed me out the door and told me never to return. Anyway, if we were to go around pointing fingers, I'd probably come out worse. There's not much point in wasting energy worrying about the injustice of it all at this stage."

"True, but let's face it, we know who we'd blame if we had the choice."

"Couldn't be anyone else could it?"

We laughed quietly, mostly to ourselves.

"Do you remember that Christmas and New Year we spent in southwest Spain?" Jane said.

"Of course, it was the end of 2017. Cassie was only four."

"Yeah, both our books had sold particularly well that year

and we were able to afford a decent holiday. Everywhere we went there were these beautiful orange trees laden with ripened fruit lining the streets, and we couldn't work out why nobody helped themselves to this abundant food source. Coming from here we couldn't understand why someone didn't just pull up a van one night and take off with the lot."

"That's right. I remember explaining to Cassie the difference between the ripe and unripe fruit and we got a bit brave. I held her up to pick one but as she went to grab it a waiter from the nearby cafe came out shouting 'not for eating, not for eating'. We didn't really know what to do and it turned into some sort of orange standoff before our Englishness took over and we sloped off sheepishly, never to go near a tree again."

Jane chuckled then said, "We became obsessed with the question of who owned the oranges for the rest of the holiday. Almost every town we passed through was the same. We used to sit in cafes watching people walk past these trees but nobody ever picked anything. Remember we came up with theories why – the whole area was covered in artificial oranges to fool tourists or the King of Spain officially owned all the fruit in the trees and only he could give permission for them to be eaten. Even Cassie got bored of us eventually. It wasn't until the last night that we found out why when we asked those guys in that cafe in Seville."

"Oh yeah, there was that drunk guy who scared Cassie because he was slamming his hand on the counter to make his point. 'The people own the oranges [slam]. They are planted by the council [slam], who harvest the oranges [slam], but the council works for us [slam] so we own the oranges [slam]'. Then we asked him why no one ate the fruit if it belonged

to the people and he said, completely straight-faced, 'because it tastes like shit', and looked at us as if we were deranged. Thankfully his friend stepped in and filled in a few of the blanks."

"Yeah, and it turned out the councils owned and maintained the trees but mostly for aesthetic reasons, harvesting the oranges every year before selling them on to be made into marmalade or something like that. People didn't eat them because they were some really bitter type of orange that was more or less inedible on its own. Essentially that drunk guy was right, even if he didn't get his point across that clearly."

"True," I said, laughing.

"It seems like the last time we were all happy together, before the country, and our lives, fell apart. In the end that's all people our age have now, memories of a better time. We may never get back what's ours, but I hope someday Cassie will."

"Me too ... it does seem like an age ago, so much has happened since then."

"I know. In fact the last twenty years or so have just disappeared. One minute poor old Gordon Brown was completing the double win of Chancellor and Prime Minister of the biggest financial fuckup in recent history, the next we woke up without the ability to vote the fucker-uppers in."

"You know, I'm fairly certain Cassie get's her occasionally colourful language from you."

"I'll probably not deny that one. Speaking of which, I better get back before detective Cassie gets home," she said, getting up to leave. "Thanks for the wine. And the chat."

"We should probably have done it more I suppose."

"Maybe, though it wouldn't make a difference to the things that are outside our control."

"I guess not. Take care of yourself," I said, embracing her at the door.

"I will," she said as she walked out the door.

A few steps out, she turned and said, "Why don't you come over for dinner some night soon?"

"Sure, that sounds great, apart from this," I said, pointing at my ankle.

"Oh. Maybe we can bring dinner to you then."

"Great. Just let me know when."

"Ok. Goodnight. Shit, it's freezing out here."

A few days later Cassie popped through the door after school.

"Hiya," she said.

"Hello Grumpy, what's up with you?"

"I'm sick of all the cruelty," she said, collapsing heavily onto the sofa next to me.

"Oh sweetie, what's happened?" I said, putting my arm around her.

"On the way over here I saw the SES grab an old man. He must have been about seventy but they just dragged him across the high street like a rubbish bag. I wanted to shout at them but I was too afraid, just like the other twenty people who walked by with their heads down."

"You did the right thing to stay out of it."

"Why? Why was that the right thing to do? What's right about two bullies hauling a defenceless man into a van? It just reminded me of everything I hate about this country."

"Cassie, I don't know what to say about it. The SES are the most physically brutal force in the country, there to compliment the mental harshness of the security service. They search out the most vicious people they can find and train them to threaten."

"But they don't just do that. I've seen the bruises on your arms. That's them isn't it?"

"Yes, but it's just handcuffs and taking me to and from their vans. If you're reasonably cooperative they won't hurt you too much."

"Fine, but what about all those people who ignored what happened on the street just now. If all of them had stood up then they would have had to stop."

"Come on, you know it's not that simple. The neighbourhood would be flooded with police and I wouldn't be the only one confined to home."

"Something has to change Dad, this can't go on. It can't be right to just ignore it and pretend there's nothing we can do."

"It isn't but powerlessness is a fact of life these days, no matter how wrong that is."

"I suppose so. I'm just not sure I can sit back and watch it happen anymore."

"You have to for now."

"Do I? Why? If everyone does nothing then everything just goes on as before."

"Come on, we've been over this already. The people with the power and money have the upper hand at the moment, however unfair that might be. That doesn't just include The Central Cabinet but their enforcers as well."

"I think I need a cup of tea," she said, getting up.

"Make me one too," I said, following her into the kitchen.

"Why do they do it?" she said as she filled up the kettle. "Why are they oblivious to everyone else's suffering?"

"I don't know," I said, sitting down at the table. "Perhaps they choose not to see it. Maybe they just don't care."

"How can that be? How can they look at the harm they inflict on other human beings and feel nothing?"

"It's not something I can claim to understand or

even empathise with. Some people just grow up not understanding the value of humanity, perhaps enjoying the authority they have over others or the financial rewards regardless of how destructive they have to be."

"It's sickening."

"It is but it's just another of those changes that happened to society over the course of a few decades. Antagonism was normalised and it's very difficult to place how and when that began. It may be the myth of aggression came first and as everyone adjusted to the idea that a certain level was normal, whether it was real or imagined, it allowed people to retreat from doing something about it, thus allowing it to expand. The point in the last few centuries of our supposedly civilised society has been that there are rules, both social and legal, that govern behaviour and a police force to safeguard that for the good of society. When you choose to subvert this and hand unaccountable power to people who have no respect for others then whatever equilibrium there was is upset. What you just saw on the street is a representation of years of people getting on with their lives in the hope that imbalance doesn't affect them. What the government forget, or choose not to see, is that if they have to use violence, hostility, anger and fear to convince people of their truth, then there's something wrong with their argument."

"How can it be normal? It's wrong to hurt people, even I know that."

"Yes but you've had to learn it and don't forget that what you're seeing now is not the average person on the street being violent, it's The Central Cabinet and their representatives. The normalisation I'm talking about relates to how people view what's happening. You could find any number of things that might explain it like how Britain's almost always been involved in some sort of war, from the Falklands in the 1980s to Iraq to the internal wars of the present day. It's become such a part of our existence that it's become an extension of national identity and an industry in itself. At a societal level the last fifty years have seen riots, football hooliganism, the internet, video games, violent movies, road rage, drunken fights and any number of other aspects of anger that were fashionably talked about and could be put forward as reasons for the acceptance of brutality, but the truth is that people just get on with their lives regardless of the chaos around them."

"I'm not sure I can do it. I don't know if I can hold it all in for much longer. I have to work out what I want to do soon but deep down I don't want to do anything here."

"Sweetie, you're going to have to do something. I know it's not a given that you'll get a decent job here but if you try you might get to a point where you can at least survive the madness."

"What, sit in one of those dreary office jobs? Turn into one of those people who'll never fight back? Conform and allow the injustice to swirl around me. I don't know if I want to be that person."

"No matter what career you choose, that's going to be how things are for the foreseeable future. You can't get away from the boring side of life. You just have to put up with it because it comes with the territory. You'll always know there's something better but for your own safety take the crappy job and keep your thoughts private until you see a way out."

"But I want to be able to do something about all of this. I want to help get rid of this system so people stop disappearing from my life."

"Sweetie, nobody's disappearing."

"Really, how can you say that for sure? Why do you think I come around here whenever I can? Every time I walk through the door I'm afraid I won't find you here, and when I haven't I come every morning and evening until you are. Someday you're not going to reappear and I'm not sure I can face that again."

"Now come on, don't think like that. I've got my tag and my occasional visitors but there's no talk of anything more permanent."

"You don't know that! Nobody does."

"Cassie, please stop talking like this."

"No, don't you get it. I'm going to do something to stop this, especially if you go. If I have to I'll sneak across the border into Scotland."

"I don't think you're thinking clearly about this. It's not as simple as that. If you're caught there's no knowing what will happen to you. It's too risky. And don't forget that the government has no problem with chasing and killing exiles and boasting about it in the media."

"So what can I do? What am I supposed to do here? I don't fit in with the way everything works."

"Sweetie, I can't answer that question for you but please be careful. Don't get involved in anything that puts you in danger. Think about your mother as well, what effect it will have on her."

"She doesn't care."

"That's definitely not true."

"Really? If she did then we'd still be a family, you wouldn't have been forced to move out and live two streets away."

"That's unfair."

"Is it? I have to live without you around because she didn't like the government coming to our door."

"Enough Cassie! You need to calm down and listen. You can't blame your mother for all this. I'm just as much to blame, if not more. Sure, I fought for a while for what I believed in, but at what cost? The reason I don't live with you anymore is my fault, not your mother's. I was the one who brought the government to our door, I was the one who gathered people in our front room to try and create some sort of resistance. I was the one who had the romantic idea that politicians who had happened on a way of sidelining democracy would listen to a bunch of writers. It was me who needed to leave so you could have some chance at a normal life without constantly having to worry about the next knock on the door."

"But I still do, it hasn't changed that fear. Now I just never see when it happens."

"I'm not saying it's turned out perfectly, but we did the best we could. We did what we thought was right to protect you. Why do you think you only use your mother's name? Mine became tainted because of the way the media smeared those who didn't agree with The Central Cabinet's actions. The main lesson I've learnt over the last ten years is keep your head down. I'm not telling you all this because I want you to try and overthrow the government. That's just not going to work right now."

She went quite for a while before saying, "I'd be proud to have your name you know."

"Oh Cassie, I know, but that's not the point. We didn't want you to have problems just because I'm your father. There was very little we could do to protect you so we did whatever we were able to."

"Moving out of home was not a little thing."

"I know it's hard to understand, but it's not like we don't see each other, or like your mother and I fight and don't speak. I suppose we saw it as a necessity, however misguided that might seem. You need to look at the wider picture Cassie, how fear grew on us in the early years of Stability. Nobody knew what might happen, especially not the journalists who had spoken out in the past. We did what we thought was best for you, and you shouldn't blame your mother for that."

"I don't really I suppose, I'm just angry ... I am a lot at the moment ... anyway, I sometimes think it was my fault all this started."

"What are you talking about?"

"When I told Miss Caulder what you said about her teaching. That's the first time the government saw you as being a problem."

"You don't really think that, do you?"

"What else could it have been?"

"Cassie, you were seven years old, you can't be held responsible for being inquisitive and you certainly can't blame yourself for everything that's happened since. To start with, she was wrong to teach you that. I was as surprised as anyone to be called into your school. That's why I wrote about it afterwards and not in a very complimentary way, but I've written a lot before and since then that's upset the authorities far more."

"Ok."

"Surely I've told you enough about this shitty system for you to understand that everything that's wrong is the fault of the people who decided that power was their right, something they should bestow on themselves and their corporate friends. That's the reason I get in trouble, nothing else. I didn't choose not to agree with them, it just wasn't possible that I ever could. Never blame yourself for the actions of a bunch of old bastards in Westminster. That isn't and could never be your fault. There's not even any point in being angry at them, they're just not worth it, and there's definitely nothing to be gained by being angry at yourself."

We sat quietly at the kitchen table, staring at the increasingly bare trees outside. A wren flew through the garden, landing to hop around not far from the patio doors, chirping loudly as it pecked at the cold grey flagstones.

"Can I stay here tonight?" Cassie said.

"I'm not sure that's such a good idea."

"Because you're due another trip around now? Don't look so surprised, if anyone knows their habits it's me. I don't care anymore, I want to spend more time with you and if that means staying here a few nights a week then that's what I'll do. You've always said the spare room is forever mine."

"Let me speak to your mother about it."

"No, I'll do it."

"Ok. She knows about these conversations we've been having by the way."

"Oh."

"Don't worry. She's fine about it, more or less."

"Ok. Good."

It was heartening to have her around for longer than the usual couple of hours. We cooked some food and watched a film, one of those bland blockbusters that so easily get through the censors.

Next morning, I was up early as always and stood in the kitchen making coffee. It chilled me as it always did when I heard the doorbell. I opened the door to find the usual squad, made up not necessarily of the same people but certainly the same type.

"Pack a bag Mr. O'Dwyer," said one of the officials.

"A bag? When have I ever needed luggage for your particular type of holiday camp?"

"Just pack it, and quickly. I recommend clothes for at least eight days, toiletries and a few personal items, which you may or may not be allowed to keep."

The realisation of what was happening came just as

Cassie appeared at the top of the stairs.

"What's going on Dad?"

"Get dressed and go home Cassie."

"Why do they want you to pack a bag?"

"Cassie. Please sweetie. Go home."

"Mr. O'Dwyer, I suggest you hurry up or we'll be forced to intervene." said the other official, indicating the four SES guards behind him.

"Ok, but you need to stay here. I want to talk to my daughter."

"I suggest you leave the door open."

"Go fuck yourself. I'll be down in a minute," I said as I slammed it shut.

I heard him order a couple of the goons around the back and a crash as they split the side gate but I wasn't stupid enough to run. I guess like everyone else who hadn't towed the line my time had come.

"Cassie," I said as I came up the stairs, "please get your things and go."

"You're not coming back this time are you?"

"We don't know that," I said, taking hold of her hands. "Look, you need to get out of here. I don't want you to be here when I leave. I don't want to give them an excuse to hassle you. I'll make sure I buy enough time for you to get home."

"Dad, please don't go."

"I don't think I have a choice. Please be quick. I'm sorry sweetie."

I made slow work of getting my bag together and when she was ready to leave I hugged her tightly.

"Take care of your mother," I said.

"I will. Someday this will all be over, won't it?"

"I hope so."

We heard a crash as the front door broke in.

"Mr. O'Dwyer, we've waited long enough," said one of the voices.

I walked downstairs with Cassie behind me.

"That was unnecessary," I said, reaching the bottom and guiding Cassie out the front door.

"I suggest you hurry up," he said before turning to Cassie. "You need to leave."

She stared at me with baffled sadness for a few moments before turning and running. I looked slowly around the living room before picking up a photo of Jane and her and walking through the splintered door to the waiting van.

The next volume of *Who owns all the oranges?* will be out in 2015.

For news sign up for email updates at www.oranburke.com

Acknowledgements

Thanks to everyone who helped with proofreading and offered suggestions, particularly Mum, Dad, Fi, Mike and Gus.

Also thanks to my tutors at City College Brighton and Hove who re-awakened a long dormant interest in journalism as an important part of democracy.

Lightning Source UK Ltd.
Milton Keynes UK
UKOW04f1214020714

234432UK00002B/21/P